"You'd better leave..." Harper murmured

Macon became utterly still. Only his breath moved, teasing her ears as he leaned nearer. "What if I don't want to?"

Gazing up at him, she suddenly couldn't pull her eyes from his mouth. A kiss would mean so little to him, she thought, craving a taste. He had a way with women; he dispensed those kisses all the time. Maybe if she had just a taste of him, she could finally forget him. Forget his lovemaking...

His voice was mesmerizing. "What if I want to stay?"

"You always did do exactly what you wanted...."

"Then I sure as hell shouldn't stop now," he drawled roughly, brushing his body against hers, the taut sweep of his hips coming with a rustle of denim. She hadn't known he was aroused, but she felt it now. He was so hard and hot and thick that her knees nearly buckled.

A moment later his mouth crushed hers and he parted her lips with the slow thrust of his tongue. Wrapping his arms tightly around her waist, he steadied her as he kicked the storm door, shutting out the summer sunlight.

He started for the bedroom and Harper was lost....

Dear Reader,

After writing many Harlequin American Romance novels, and stories for other Harlequin series, it's been pure fun to approach my thirtieth book by shifting gears and trying some especially spicier, steamier stories, so I hope you'll enjoy this, as well as my upcoming BIG APPLE BACHELORS trilogy for Temptation.

Usually when I daydream about mail-order men, I think of gorgeous guys arriving from far-off foreign lands with the sole intention of sweeping me off my feet and pleasuring me senseless, but this time the fantasy got a little more complex.

When sexy rancher Macon McCann receives no responses from his mail-order-bride ad, he's stunned to discover that the local postmistress, his ex-lover whom he's been avoiding for years, has actually been opening his mail and writing women back, telling them not to come to Texas because he's such a bad catch!

I hope you will be amused by the shenanigans that follow, especially watching a woman get repeatedly swept off her feet and pleasured senseless by somebody she keeps swearing she can't stand. Of course, she really loves Macon, and I hope you will, too.

Happy reading,

Jule McBride

Books by Jule McBride

HARLEQUIN TEMPTATION
761—A BABY FOR THE BOSS

HARLEQUIN AMERICAN ROMANCE
733—AKA: MARRIAGE
753—SMOOCHIN' SANTA
757—SANTA SLEPT OVER
849—SECRET BABY SPENCER

A WAY WITH WOMEN
Jule McBride

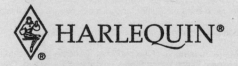

TORONTO • NEW YORK • LONDON
AMSTERDAM • PARIS • SYDNEY • HAMBURG
STOCKHOLM • ATHENS • TOKYO • MILAN • MADRID
PRAGUE • WARSAW • BUDAPEST • AUCKLAND

For Birgit Davis-Todd,
whose patient nurturing of writers has produced
years of Temptations: whole worlds, new loves,
teary laughter and sweet emotion,
so many hours of delight and pleasure.
As both a reader and writer, thanks.

ISBN 0-373-25930-1

A WAY WITH WOMEN

Copyright © 2001 by Julianne Moore.

This edition published by arrangement with Harlequin Books S.A.

Visit us at www.eHarlequin.com

Printed in U.S.A.

_____Prologue_____

"MACON MCCANN'S STILL advertising for a bride? Some things simply shouldn't be allowed," Harper Moody said under her breath. Shrugging out of a navy postal uniform blazer, she rolled up the sleeves of a standard-issue white blouse, raked her shoulder-length ash hair into a ponytail and secured it with a string tie the U.S. government had meant for use around her neck. Ponytail in place, she sipped the scalding coffee she'd bought at Go-Mart and glanced over as her sole customer, Lois Potts from Potts Feed and Seed, paced between padded Jiffy bags and dusty express envelopes, trying to decide between the John Wayne commemorative stamps or the City Flag series.

Lois was the last person Harper wanted to deal with, of course, since she and Lois had a history. Fortunately, the other woman was occupied, so Harper stared down again, first at a box of pink stationary she'd gotten when she bought the coffee, then at *Texas Men* magazine. "I really can't believe they let Macon advertise for a bride," she mumbled. "The fine print assures they screen these guys."

Her fog-blue eyes drifted down the full-body photo of the man who'd fathered her teenage son. *One hundred percent pure rich rancher stud*, announced the caption. "Macon *would* come up with a line like that," she whispered, rolling her eyes and feeling distressed by her physical response to him.

Well, what female wouldn't react?

Muscles tested the shoulder seams of a denim shirt Macon wore unsnapped, exposing tangled chest hairs the color of sunlit wheat. His broad chest slimmed to narrow hips and slightly bowed legs whose long strides were usually headed in the opposite direction from Harper. Boot-cut jeans flared over his polished boots, and Macon was clutching a Stetson against his chest, smiling ruefully as if to say every female answering the ad had already broken his heart.

"Angel's hair on the very devil," she pronounced with annoyance. The honey-colored waves framing Macon's broad, inviting face called to her fingertips to test their silky texture.

Well, she assured herself, placing her steaming coffee cup on the postal scale, Macon just looked like any other dumb cowboy—except for his eyes. As sharp as spurs, they were aware and intense, their color the aged amber of the house ale he'd been enjoying every Saturday night at Big Grisly's Grill since he'd come back to town.

The wayward drift of her eyes ventured below a turquoise-studded belt, landing on jeans as soft as kid gloves. Just like a good love story, the fit was loose enough to leave room for imagination, but revealing enough to assure a woman of a happy ending. Glancing away, Harper realized she could recall plenty about Macon that no camera could capture. "Yeah, me—and every other female in Pine Hills," she huffed. Nevertheless, Macon's hands—the same lean-fingered bronzed hands that clutched the Stetson over his heart—had left their imprints on Harper, and once a woman knew certain things about a man, there was no turning back. She knew plenty, too. Including that Macon had fathered a son he didn't know about. *My son, Cordy.*

Harper steadied herself by taking another careful sip of scalding coffee. Years ago, she'd done the right thing in not telling Macon about Cordy, but now she'd come to fear something terrible might happen to her. Bruce's death two years ago proved unexpected, horrible things *did* happen. What if, after she was gone, Cordy needed to know the truth for some reason? What if he became ill and needed a bone marrow transplant or a blood transfusion or he had a car wreck or...?

She pushed down the fear that had gnawed at her ever since Bruce died and thought, *Damn you, Bruce, we were supposed to get old together! You weren't supposed to die!* No more than Macon McCann was supposed to settle down in Pine Hills with a woman he was meeting through the U.S. mail.

Macon had become a successful contractor in Houston. Why would he come home now? And why was he advertising for a wife in *Texas Men* magazine when he had ample opportunities to date?

Shifting her gaze, Harper distracted herself by glancing past the metal detector, copiers and post-office boxes through the front door. Heat baked the sidewalks, and although it was only mid-morning, folks were already lined up four-deep inside Happy Lick's Ice Cream Parlor. Outside, white-hot sun was melting everything from the cream in waffle cones to the rubber on truck tires.

"Morning, Harper. How's it going?"

It was Lois. Harper scooted an express envelope over Macon's ad, as well as over the other items she'd spread on the counter, then she lifted her coffee cup from the postal scale so Lois could weigh a package. "Fine, Lois. No stamps today?"

"Couldn't decide what kind." Lois nodded at the help wanted sign. "I see you're looking for new blood."

As heiress to Potts Feed and Seed, Lois hardly needed a job, but Harper found herself worrying, fearing Lois, for some harebrained reason, would apply. "Hmm," commented Harper. "It would have been cheaper to send my coffee than your package."

Lois chuckled appreciatively. "Guess you heard Macon McCann's back in town and dating everything that moves. Weren't you friends in high school?"

Lois, of course, was one of the things that moved. "Just platonic," Harper lied.

"Same here," assured Lois.

Harper suppressed a snort of laughter. "I heard you two went bowling last week over in Opossum Creek." Harper couldn't help but counter, realizing news of Macon's *Texas Men* ad hadn't yet hit town and wondering if she should tell Lois, who'd be sure to spread the word. No man would want it known that he'd stooped to advertising for a wife, and if Macon was embarrassed enough, maybe Harper would get lucky and he'd leave Pine Hills for good.

"Macon and I did go to Opossum Creek," Lois clarified before moving on to other gossip. "But we were with a group."

Only Harper's raised eyebrow contradicted her. After she checked out, Lois ambled to the stamps for another look and Harper stared out the window, her gaze following South Dallas, the main drag of town. Flat as a ruler for miles, the road snaked like a ribbon when it reached Pine Cone Mountain. Farther up, blacktop turned into red dirt and dead-ended at a parking spot called Star Point. Maybe if the only movie screen in Pine Hills showed first-run rather than retro movies, or if the nearest bowling alley wasn't forty miles away in Opossum Creek, or if Happy Lick's Ice Cream Parlor didn't close promptly at eight p.m., Harper wouldn't have spent quite so many nights sneaking up there with Macon.

But Star Point had been irresistible, heaven on earth, with shady live oaks, mesquites and sycamores that cooled you even in the worst dog days of August. Miles from town, stars glittered like diamonds on black velvet in a jewelry store, looking so close that Harper always felt sure she could touch them. Atop that distant hill, so close to the stars—and just two months before Harper married Bruce—she and Macon made their baby.

Now she stared critically at Macon's photo and reread the advertisement. "Thirty-four-year-old Texas cowboy wants to marry. Man comes complete with successful cattle ranch in Texas Hill Country and promises his bride her very own horse to ride."

Feeling testy, Harper crossed her arms. "He makes Pine Hills sound like 'Little House on the Prairie,'" she muttered, pitying any poor, misinformed woman who might fall for the John Boy Walton routine. "At least until she meets him," Harper whispered. "A horse," she added, shaking her head. "Half the people in Texas don't even know how to ride, so if some woman's fool enough to marry you, Macon, why not just break down and give her a four-wheel drive?"

Lois was pushing through the door, on her way out. "Did you say something, Harper?"

Blushing, Harper shook her head. "Just talking to myself."

"It's only a problem when you start answering," quipped Lois before the door closed.

The last thing Harper needed right now was words of wisdom from Lois Potts, but she politely nodded acknowledgment, then continued reading. "So, here's the offer, ladies. Come to the Rock 'n' Roll Ranch in Pine Hills, Texas, and be lulled by nature's peace while you fall in love with both me and the old west. Enjoy the slow pace, deer and armadillos, hike the paths and fish and swim in the ponds. We've got a swimming pool, and I hope you love family atmosphere because you'll be sharing a spacious rustic ranch house with your in-laws, Cam and Blanche McCann. So, write Macon McCann soon. This cowboy's ready to be your loving husband now. But don't forget, it's first come, first served."

It didn't make sense. Macon had left Pine Hills sixteen years ago to pursue his dreams—and he'd never looked back. He'd never shown signs of marrying, either. And he wouldn't marry a stranger, would he? Why, when he had so many dates?

Harper's throat tightened as she edged aside the express envelope so she could look at the letters she'd stacked beside *Texas Men*. Sixteen responses to Macon's advertisement had arrived this morning from all over the world. Most days, there were even more. *It's a simple process,* she'd told herself this morning as she always did. *Lift letter from mail pouch. Open post office box for Macon McCann. Place letter from wannabe bride into Macon McCann's mailbox. Close mailbox.*

Simple, yes. But Harper simply couldn't force herself to give Macon the letters from all those women. Instead, she'd steamed them open and begun to read. Some letters made her laugh, some brought the sting of unshed tears to her eyes. Women had written from as far away as China, Russia and the Netherlands; all told stories of parents, lovers or husbands they wanted to leave, of war-torn countries from which they were desperate to escape or poverty-stricken conditions from which they sought refuge. They said they wanted a husband to help raise their children, or they wanted a taste of ranch life, but what they really wanted was somebody to love and somebody to love them back.

On a raw pull of feeling, Harper lifted a letter written painstakingly on wide-rule notebook paper. Youthfully rounded purple cursive letters looped in flourishes; large circles dotted the *i*s.

Dear Mr. Macon McCann,
Your ranch sounds real pretty, and I want very much to be your bride. I promise I'm a nice per-

son, from a good Christian home, but my family is
mad at me right now because I got pregnant by accident. I thought of other options, but I'm going to
keep this baby even though my boyfriend was lying when he said he loved me. I'm scared. I'm only
seventeen, and we don't have a lot of money since
my daddy's a shoeshine man at the airport. Please,
Mr. McCann, if you don't have anything against
marrying an African American girl who's just
dropped out of school and is going to have a baby
in two months, I hope you'll write me soon. I hate
my family right now and want to move away from
Missouri. Even though I used to make straight As
in school, I had to drop out because the girls I
thought were my friends aren't my friends anymore. They taped mean notes on my locker door.
Isn't it weird that the name of my home state
"Missouri" sounds just like the word "misery?"
Because that's how I feel right now, just miserable,
Mr. McCann. Please help me.

    I know it's too soon to say it, but I will, anyway,

Love, your future bride,

Chantal Morris

How selfish could Macon be? Harper wondered.
Didn't he realize he was leading on confused young
girls who had nowhere to turn? Chantal Morris, like so
many others who'd written since Macon placed the ad,
was undoubtedly frightened out of her mind, and if
she wasn't careful, she might actually find herself at
the mercy of Macon.

Which meant Harper'd better talk some sense into Chantal. After all—Harper lifted her eyes toward Star Point—she had been even younger than Chantal, only sixteen, when she and Macon conceived. Harper mulled over how many women he'd dated since his return from Houston—everybody from the new schoolteacher, Betsy, who was from Idaho, and Lois Potts, not to mention Nancy Ludell, a notorious gossip who lived at the end of Harper's road and who was newly divorced and sticking to Macon like white on rice.

"Chantal Morris needs to graduate," Harper whispered. "She's not that much older than my son, and without her diploma, it'll be even harder for her to take care of a baby."

Tapping a pen against Chantal's letter, Harper wondered how to help. Tampering with the U.S. mail was a federal offense, of course, but Harper was on the school board, and her donations did help outfit the Pine Hills Armadillos football team. Surely, she thought, the town fathers would help keep her out of prison if Macon ever got wind of what she was doing. Besides, fate would protect her, since her motives were pure. No, Chantal wasn't the first misguided, underage girl who mistakenly thought she wanted to marry Macon. Harper had once made that mistake herself.

She reread Chantal's letter slowly, frowning over every word, and then, assuring herself she was doing her civic duty, she lifted a sheet from the stationary

box. The paper was pink and bubble-gum scented—
that was unfortunate—but Chantal wouldn't mind.
Nor would the other women with whom Harper intended to correspond, sharing her experience, strength
and hope concerning Macon. Shutting her eyes, Harper waited for inspiration and then began to write:

Dear Chantal,
From personal experience, I can imagine what a
bad time you're having in Missouri, so I hope
you'll take my advice: finish high school! You
won't regret keeping your baby, and your diploma will be of great help in the future. I gave
birth to my baby just after I turned seventeen, and
being a young mom was fun. Now, I wouldn't
have the energy! I'm thirty-three now, and this au-
tumn my son is starting eleventh grade. For years,
he's been my greatest source of happiness. I know
it will be the same for you. The right man will
come along, so my advice is to stay strong. Don't
let those awful girls at school get you down.
You've got to finish high school, have your baby
and hold out for the man of your dreams!

Lifting the pen, Harper bit down on her lower lip as if
that might stop the sudden lurch of her heart. Because
she'd been double promoted, Harper had been
younger than the other girls at school and, like Chantal, she hadn't had many friends. She'd loved her husband—Harper really had—and yet... Cutting off the
thought, she assured herself that what she'd felt for

Macon had been girlish infatuation. She continued writing.

> Chantal, fortunately for you, I'm reviewing the *Texas Men* respondents for Mr. McCann. You have a wonderful future ahead of you—I can feel it in my bones, sweetheart. But, believe me, that future is not in Pine Hills, Texas. Macon McCann is not the man for you, nor would he be a good father for your—or anyone else's—baby....

1

MACON MCCANN'S soft drawl moved through the ranch office like a mountain cat stalking prey, sounding slow, purposeful and ready to pounce. "I should have guessed our local postmistress was behind this."

Diego, the ranch's cow boss, paced thoughtfully, wiping sweat from his brow with a bandanna. "Shoulda, woulda, coulda."

Three words that definitely pertained to himself and the widow Moody, Macon thought. Being railroaded by his father into advertising for a bride was bad enough, but when no hopefuls even answered his invitation in *Texas Men*, Macon should have gotten suspicious. At first, he'd even considered renting a second P.O. box, to accommodate all the mail he'd expected. Oh, he prided himself on having no foolish illusions, but Macon'd figured *some* women would be excited by the prospect of cooking and cleaning at the new house he wanted to build on the ranch.

In order to facilitate the process, Macon had sent *Texas Men* a picture. No problem there. He was better-looking than most men in the magazine. Wealthier, too.

But nobody answered the ad.

And now the mystery was solved. "Harper Moody," Macon murmured, hell-bent on not letting his true emotions show. Leaning back, he crossed his boots on a scarred wood desk and stared down dispassionately at the pink sheets he'd taken from Harper's work station at the post office an hour ago. Not even the aroma of hay and horses overpowered the bubble-gum scent wafting from the sheets, and Macon found it particularly bothersome since beneath that, he imagined he could smell a scent he preferred to forget.

Harper's scent.

Since she handled every piece of mail passing through Pine Hills, Macon should have known she'd see his ad and do something to thwart him, but had she really opened the respondents' letters and corresponded with his potential brides?

The screen door breezed open, and Macon glanced up to see his father, Cam, come inside with Ansel Walters, who owned the ranch bordering the Rock 'n' Roll. "The moment Macon advertised for a wife," Ansel joked, glancing between the letters and Diego and Cam, "he expected to see those brides come a runnin'."

"Like on that old TV show, 'Here Comes the Brides'," added Diego, his sparkling eyes as black and shiny as the curls sticking from beneath his battered straw hat. "Yes, indeed," Diego continued as he stripped a sweat-soaked shirt from his middle-aged, wiry frame, folded it over the back of a swivel chair and plopped down with a grunt. "Every woman in the world be desperate to get herself hitched to a rich rancher stud like Macon, right, Macon?"

"Just ask any female," Cam added as he tossed his work gloves next to the letters. "Marrying my son's their main goal in life. You boys wouldn't *believe* how many brides I had to fight past to get to work this morning!"

Macon shot his father a quelling glance.

Cam laughed. "Oh, c'mon, don't get mad, Macon. I never told you to advertise for a bride."

"No, you didn't," Macon said, worriedly running a hand over his head, slicking back the gold waves. "But you said you won't legally hand the ranch over to me until I'm married."

"Now you're catching on." Cam's left hand was nearly immobile, due to a stroke he'd suffered, but he gleefully clapped the other on his knee. "I don't want you running the Rock 'n' Roll yet. It's my ranch, and no matter what your ma says, I'm not retiring."

Macon surveyed his father a long moment, his gut clenching as if he'd been punched. Cam's shoulders, once as powerful as Macon's, were thin and stooped, and what was left of his hair had turned bristly gray. His face was as wrinkled as a pair of old boots, and suddenly, noticing how his father had changed with age, Macon wished he'd never left home. He missed the years he hadn't been here, working the ranch with Cam. Macon had been a late baby, the only child, and now Cam was seventy-three.

Harper, why did you make me leave?

And where had the years gone? Only yesterday, the woman he'd wanted had been in his arms. Only the day before that, he'd been knock-kneed and in short pants, chasing after Cam in the fields. *Pa, when you gonna teach me to ride that big horse? When you gonna take me to herd cattle? When you gonna let me rope a bull?* And now he was hearing his mother's voice. *I can't talk sense into him, Macon. His blood pressure's sky-high, and if he doesn't get some help with the ranch, he'll have another stroke. Doc Dickens says so.* Blanche McCann might as well have said, *Your father's going to die if you don't come home, Macon.*

Nothing less could have brought Macon to Pine Hills, since the last place he wanted to live was in the same town as Harper. He said, "Doc says you've got to retire on account of your blood pressure."

"The only pressure I've got is you trying to take away my ranch," muttered Cam. "Fortunately, every woman in the world's got the sense not to marry you."

"If I get married, you retire," Macon said. "You promised."

"And Cam never goes back on his word," said Ansel.

"Nope, I don't," agreed Cam. "But somehow I doubt I'll hear church bells, since Harper wrote every woman in China, just to warn them about Macon."

"And every woman in Pine Hills already knows better than to get involved with him," added Ansel.

"Now, now," chided Cam. "Nancy Ludell's still trying. And that cute schoolteacher, Betsy, who moved down from Idaho. And Ansel's wife's best friend... what'sername?"

"Lois Potts," Ansel supplied.

"Right. You went bowling with her," Cam coaxed, his tone insinuating. "Why, Lois is the closest thing we've got to an heiress in Pine Hills, since she'll inherit the Feed and Seed. Why not marry her?"

"I *might* marry Lois," Macon muttered, though marrying a stranger would be just as good an option. Macon wasn't necessarily looking to fall in love. He wasn't even sure if he was capable of it anymore.

Ansel suddenly whirled around, shielded his eyes and squinted through a smudged window at the corral. "Hurry, Macon!" he teased. "Some women in wedding dresses are running this way!"

Diego ran to the door. "Look at them wild womens lifting their veils just so they can claw out each other's eyes! They's fighting over Macon like cats and dogs." The Mexican raised his voice to a falsetto. "Please, please," he crooned, twining a finger around the end of a black mustache, "let me marry Macon and iron his shirts and give him some good lovin'!"

"Back off," warned Macon mildly. Suddenly, he yawned and stretched his powerful arms over his head. Damn it *all*—his father, Harper and the cattle, too. Late last night, over a hundred head had broken through a pasture onto Ansel's property, so Macon had been mending fences since before sunup, stopping only to run into town to check the mail, which was how he'd discovered the letters.

Diego squinted. "What's those letters say about how bad you is, anyway?"

Macon shrugged, lifting a pink, bubble-gum scented sheet. "'Dear Gong Zhu,'" Macon drawled, ignoring the tightening of his chest as he took in Harper's neat cursive, "'It's in your best interest to know there are good reasons Macon McCann has to advertise for a bride. Think about it. What kind of American man has to go all the way to China just to get a girlfriend?'"

Ansel, Diego and Cam chuckled.

Macon stirred the letters with a finger. "Here's another. 'Dear Carrie Dawn Bledscoe, Please know that Pine Hills, Texas has a male-female ratio of three to one. If Macon McCann was such a great catch, don't you think a local girl would have married him by now? He's thirty-four, so they've had ample opportunity.'"

The men laughed, and despite his underlying anger, a smile tugged at Macon's lips. "Get this," he added. "She signs the letter, 'Yours in female solidarity.'"

Ansel snorted. "That woman's sure got a way with words."

It's not all she's got a way with, Ansel. "This one gets right to the point," continued Macon. "'Dear Anna Gonzales, Do not come to America! Stay in Mexico and away from Macon McCann. He's a menace, and Pine Hills is one big dusty dive. There's no rain, and the heat's insufferable. Pine Hills,'" continued Macon, fishing for another letter, "'sounds uneventful, right? Well, guess what, Mirabella Morehead. When it comes to wildlife, Macon's only the beginning. Unlike in Los Angeles, we've got more than our fair share of poisonous snakes. No culture, either. You won't find first-run movies, or musical events.'"

"She's got a point." Diego swiped away tears of laughter. "The only music we gots is from frogs and crickets."

"It's nobody's fault but hers if she hates it," argued Ansel. "She could have left town. Both she and her mama said she planned to. She skipped a grade, and she had a scholarship to some Eastern school."

"She stayed to antagonize Macon," Cam guessed.

"Which is why I moved to Houston," said Macon,

despite the fact that no man present really understood how serious he'd once been about Harper.

"Well, amigo—" Diego looked sympathetic "—now you're back. And the only thing standing between you and this ranch is Harper."

Ansel grinned. "A formidable force."

Restless and tired of the ribbing, Macon rose, crossed the room and leaned in the door frame, staring through the screen at the rock bluffs and green hills that had given the Rock 'n' Roll Ranch its name. He watched corralled horses grazing under the shade trees. *Why can't you just leave me alone, Harper?*

When he decided to advertise in *Texas Men*, his motive had been purely business, but when no one wrote back, Macon had felt an unexpected void and admitted the truth to himself. He wanted a wife. He'd tried for years to get over Harper. He'd waited long enough. Didn't he deserve to start waking in the night with someone beside him, each inch of her his for the touching? *She'd* had a man's warm body beside her for sixteen years. *She'd* enjoyed shared morning kisses and raising a son. Hundreds of protective miles no longer lay between him and Harper, and Macon needed to have a woman with him, if only to prove to Harper that he still could.

She was thirty-three now and probably nothing like the girl he'd left behind, but physical distance and the passage of time had never deadened Macon's feelings the way he'd hoped. Some Christmases, he'd run into her, Bruce and their son, Cordy, and every time, something inside Macon would curl up and die. He'd tighten his arm around whatever woman he happened to be entertaining, intimating plenty more was going on than there ever really was, then he'd return to Houston. Oh, he'd tried other relationships, but nothing ever panned out. He'd missed Pine Hills, too, but couldn't live in the same town as her.

But now Bruce was dead, and Macon was here to stay.

He'd offered a quick hello in the post office before he and Harper reached a silent, mutual agreement not to exchange pleasantries. Since then, he'd wordlessly checked the mail, never venturing past the copiers in the lobby, but always aware of Harper behind the counter.

Today, she'd hung a paper clock over the counter, next to a help wanted sign, indicating she'd be gone for five minutes, so after he'd checked the empty P.O. box, Macon had given in to the impulse to glance into her work space. He'd been stunned to find Harper's unmailed responses to his brides. Wanting time to process how she'd been disparaging him, he'd grabbed the letters and left.

But what had possessed her? She had no right to stand between him and a woman. She'd married. As much as he liked her son, Cordy, who'd been working odd summer jobs on the Rock 'n' Roll since around the time Bruce died, Macon still hated the fact that she'd had him by another man. Macon knew he'd satisfied her sexually but figured Bruce had offered Harper another, better kind of sharing, touching her in a way so deep she'd married him. Macon tried to ignore the words teasing the edges of his consciousness. *Why couldn't it be me, Harper? Why wouldn't you let me break the iron grip your mama had on you?*

Macon's lips compressed. He had no choice but to confront her about the letters, but he hadn't wanted to create a scene at the post office, since it was the gossip hub of Pine Hills, and now he wasn't sure he could handle being inside the house she'd shared with Bruce. Being anywhere near the bed where she'd given herself to her husband made Macon as tense as he'd been years ago when he'd caught his first glimpse of her.

She'd been sixteen and headed to live with relatives in Tuscaloosa when her mama's car broke down in Pine Hills. One thing led to another and they'd stayed. Harper's mama got a job managing a Laundromat, where Harper spent every day after school when she wasn't sneaking off with Macon. Now he figured there wasn't a landmark in town where he hadn't made out with her, in the old cemetery, the rock quarry and on the sloping banks of Star Point Lake. Even Ansel, with whom Macon had been thick as thieves since birth, didn't know how much time he'd spent with Harper, since her mama was so strict that they'd kept their meetings as secret as possible.

Her mama had died the year before Bruce had, but Macon had never stopped hating the woman. She'd had her suspicions about what Macon and Harper were doing, and anytime she saw Macon in town, she'd pull him aside, her blue eyes narrow and fierce and her voice cracking from the Camels she chainsmoked. *My baby girl's smarter than you. She don't need your kind. You and me know you're just using her, trying to*

get the one thing boys want. But she's got herself one of those
scholarships, so the last thing she needs is you.

Macon had been young and rebellious enough that
he could have told the woman what he thought of her,
but he hadn't, out of respect for Harper. In her own
way, Macon guessed the woman had loved Harper.
And loving Harper, at least, was something Macon understood.

But she'd turned out to be her mama's girl all the
way. She'd rebelled, but not before that twisted
woman had filled her head with dire warnings about
men, just because she was backward and because a
man had left *her* when *she* was pregnant with Harper.
The summer they were out of school, Macon begged
Harper to leave home and run away with him, and
she'd finally said she would.

That night, he'd waited in the truck under a canopy
of trees not far from Big Grisly's Grill, alternately peering down the road and staring into a night as starry as
Harper's eyes. *Where are you?* he'd thought with panic.
Don't stand me up. Don't let your mama win.

But she had.

And then she'd married Bruce and given birth to
Cordy. Now Macon lifted his gaze from the horses in
the corral, realizing he'd been half admiring their
dreamless ease, their thoughtless pleasure. Why
couldn't *his* life be that damn simple? "What?"

Diego's black eyes narrowed. "Stewing about the
widow?"

Macon shook his head. "Just hoping that new
fence'll hold."

"Don't let her get you down," said Ansel. "You saw

her son, Cordy, last Saturday when he came over here to help herd cattle. He's ready to leave the nest, so Harper's just looking for distractions. She's like her own crazy mama, always meddling." Ansel frowned. "Wait a minute. Back in high school, was there more going on with you and Harper than we knew about?"

Plenty. "'Course not." Crossing to the desk, Macon stared at big block letters that stated: "Everything you read in *Texas Men* magazine is a lie. Here is the real Macon McCann." Attached was a photo of a grizzled, leather-faced, bearded man three times Macon's age. Macon held up the photograph, forcing a smile. "This guy makes Cam look pretty."

Cam laughed. "Don't take your love troubles out on me, son."

"They're not love troubles," Macon grumbled, wishing his father would simply turn over the ranch to him. Since he wouldn't unless Macon married, Macon had no choice but to fix things so the *Texas Men* respondents could write him back.

Macon snuggled his hat down on his head and after a moment's hesitation dug in a pocket for the keys to his truck. "I reckon I'd better head over to the Moodys'," he explained. He tried to tell himself that he no longer felt betrayed or cared that she hadn't loved him. Things just hadn't worked out. Still, Harper had no right to open his mail, and the words she'd written to Chantal Morris played in his mind. *Hold out for the man of your dreams.... Macon McCann is not the man for you, nor would he be a good father for your—or anyone else's—baby....*

How had Harper known what kind of father he'd

make? She'd never given him a chance. "Figure I'd better go over there," he repeated gruffly. "At least give her a piece of my mind."

"Careful that's all you give her a piece of," Ansel warned.

"Careful you don't start makin' bacon, Macon!" added Diego.

Cam cupped a hand around his ear. "You hear that sizzling sound, Diego? You smell something burning?"

"Hooee," hooted Diego. "It's Macon. He's hotter 'n chili peppers on a branding iron."

Macon set his lips grimly, bracing himself for the sparks that always flew between him and Harper. Fact was, in the old days, he and Harper's explosive arguments *had* always landed them in bed—or more likely the floor, or a bed of pine needles, or the back seat of the nearest available vehicle. But it had been years since they'd shared that unbridled lust. *Then*, they couldn't keep their hands off each other. *Then*, the resolution to any heated exchange was reached only one way—with her undressed and Macon hot and heavy between her legs.

But that was then, and this was now.

And now, stepping through the screen door into the scorching Texas heat, Macon assured himself he could confront her at her house without incident.

Now, everything was going to be different.

2

"HERE COMES TROUBLE," Harper whispered, pressing her fingertips to the door screen, her heart hammering as Macon's red pickup truck came down her tree-lined road. She never should have left her work station today to freshen up. Leave it to *him* to check his P.O. box while she was finger combing her hair and experimenting with eyeshadows. She hadn't worn makeup since Bruce died, but now Macon was back in town, and she didn't want him to think she wasn't aging well.

This would teach her.

Earlier, she'd returned to the mail counter to find the lobby empty and Macon pushing through the door, pink stationery fisted in his hand. She'd quickly hunkered guiltily behind a display until he was out of sight.

As Macon now nosed his truck beneath the willow tree that served as her carport, Harper reminded herself that she had nothing to fear. In fact, she should take great pleasure in telling Macon the truth about why she'd written to all those women.

Macon got out of the truck and slammed the door. Pretending he wasn't aware she was staring at him from behind the screen, he glanced around the yard, his gaze resting momentarily on an old sandbox. Harper hadn't removed it, compelled, she supposed, by the same maternal force that made her hold on to Cordy's craft class artwork, skateboard and first mountain bike. She watched anxiously as Macon casually assessed the house, taking in the sweeping, white-railed wraparound porch, porch swing and petunias spilling from the weathered pine flower boxes Bruce had built.

When their eyes met, her fingertips curled on the door screen as if the flat surface could provide her with support. All at once, she couldn't think straight or breathe, and she kept trying to swallow, but she couldn't do that, either. She wished Cordy was home, then she felt guilty for wanting to use her teenager— *my and Macon's teenager*, she thought with breathless panic—to shield her from his own father. It was wishful thinking, anyway, since Cordy was gone, spending the night with his best friend.

Breathe, she coached herself as Macon approached. It should have been easy, but just like delivering Macon's mail from all those women, it wasn't. Besides, she was too busy worrying about the bags only she noticed under her eyes, and about how, after her thirtieth birthday, cellulite had dappled her thighs overnight while every other inch of her started leaning like the Tower of Pisa.

Macon, of course, had never looked better.

Why did *he* have to be the one man about whom her mama had been so right? And why did seeing him in her front yard hurt so much even after all these years? Well, no matter what, she wouldn't allow her anger to surface. What was past was past. Besides, any show of passion around Macon—even temper—might lead them places neither was prepared to go.

It was the wrong time to remember their lovemaking had been too urgent for them to ever make it as far as a bed. Or to realize Macon had showered and changed since coming to the post office. He was wearing fresh jeans and a pressed white short-sleeved, snap-up shirt, and despite that she was bracing herself for battle, he looked even better than he did in *Texas Men* magazine. For the briefest second, she thought he'd changed clothes for her, then she recalled it was Friday night and Macon probably had a date. She felt a rush of temper.

He came up the porch stairs lifting off his Stetson and stopping wordlessly on the other side of the door, staring at her through the screen, his amber eyes touched with barely suppressed anger. His hair was a delicious mess, the rich gold waves rippling in early evening sunlight that slanted across the wide planks of the porch.

"Harper," he drawled, the hard consonants of her name lost so that it might have been something else entirely, such as Apa or Happa.

"Macon," she returned just as calmly. It was the first time she'd spoken his name aloud to him since he'd come home, and doing so did such funny things to her heartbeat that she shot an involuntary glance over her shoulder, as if Bruce was still alive and might catch her out here alone with another man. Just looking at Macon McCann made her feel *that* guilty.

"We need to talk, Harper."

Thankfully, the screen was safely between her and

Macon. Everything inside her was tightening as it did whenever he got this close. It would be impossible to convince herself that the heat suffusing her skin was anything other than pure lust, but she tried, assuring herself that nothing could be as brutally punishing as this god-awful Texas heat. "Talk? About...?"

"You know why I'm here." Pulling a sheet of crumpled pink bubble-gum scented stationery from his back pocket, Macon waved it in her direction, then repocketed it. "Mind if I come in?"

She considered, nervously lifting a hand to smooth her hair, his penetrating glance making her conscious that she'd brushed it up into a loose topknot, just the way he liked it, leaving long stray sexy wisps curling against her neck. She'd put on a strappy white sundress embroidered with bluebonnets, too, which showed plenty of cleavage. Licking her lips against their sudden dryness, she assured herself she'd only dressed this way because of the heat. Blowing out a shaky sigh, she said, "No, you'd better not come in."

Macon didn't bother to ask why not. He knew why not. He considered the matter even longer than she had. "Yeah," he finally said. "Okay. I guess you're right. I'd better not." After a moment, his eyes locked on hers with an intensity that made her shudder. "Aren't you coming out here then?"

His perusal was sapping strength from all her joints, so she wasn't sure she could step over the threshold if she tried. "I don't think I'd better come out, either."

Losing patience, he raised an eyebrow in question. "So, you're going to stay in there, barricading the door?"

"I'm not," she defended on a rush of pique. "But *should* I be barricading my door? Am I in trouble?"

Since they were nose to nose, it was definitely a good thing the screen was between them. "I'm not here to have a battle of wits, Harper."

She couldn't help but flash him a quick smile even though her stomach felt awfully jittery—probably from all the coffee she'd drank this morning. "Wouldn't a *battle* require *two* people with wits, Macon?"

"As ever," he retorted, "your tongue's sharp as spurs."

She couldn't quite believe how quickly she'd lost control of the conversation, and yet her heart tugged as she thought of the letters she'd read this morning. All those women were in such trouble. "In this day and age, a woman had better be sharp," she said pointedly.

"Especially if she's tampering with the U.S. mail."

"You didn't have to come here. You could have simply called the sheriff, Macon."

"And have you arrested? I thought of that myself, and it's sorely tempting, but there's more than just you to worry about. Did you think of that, Harper?"

Hearing him say her name made her heart skip a beat, but she ignored that and squinted through the screen. "Think of what?"

"Of Cordy. Your son. He's a good kid. I'd hate to see him minus a mother, which is where he'll be if I call the sheriff and you go to jail."

For a second, she ceased to breathe. As far as she knew Cordy and Macon had been introduced—on the rare occasions she'd run into Macon, Cordy had sometimes been with her—but Macon had said Cordy's name so familiarly, almost as if their relationship were personal. Knowing she should feel more relief about Macon not taking legal action, she managed to say, "You're letting me off the hook? Don't tell me you found a heart in Houston."

He stared at her a long moment, his expression bemused and faintly accusatory, as if *she'd* somehow wronged *him*. "I always *had* a heart, Harper."

As if she didn't. Nervously, she scraped a thumbnail on the screen. "If you don't intend to take any action, why'd you come over?"

His gaze flickered over her dainty dress, his voice lowering with a huskiness he was obviously trying to fight. The barely heard words were rough, but there was no mistaking the innuendo. "Do you *want* me to take some sort of action, Harper?"

She imagined she knew exactly what type of action he meant. "Of course not!"

Eyeing her dress, he didn't look convinced. Only when he touched the screen did she realize she was still running her thumbnail across it. His fingertip brushed her thumb through the metal, the touch lasting just long enough to assure her there was still an electrical spark between them. "Please," he muttered, "could you stop that? It's driving me crazy."

She couldn't help but say, "Maybe I like driving you crazy."

Everything about him seemed to still at her words. He frowned. "I came over because what you did is wrong, Harper. You know that."

Yes, and she also knew that if he studied her neck

any harder where the pulse was beating out of control, she'd lose her self-control. "*You* should be illegal."

"I'll take that as a compliment."

Silently, she stared at him, cursing that sudden teasing lift at the corners of a mouth that kept reminding her of how well he kissed. She'd meant to fight how his voice always dropped directly into her bloodstream with a dark ripple, but here she was—heart racing, hamstrings quivering, shaky all over. Trying to regain her equilibrium, she lifted her chin a notch. "It wasn't meant as a compliment."

"No? Then how'd you mean it?"

Having no answer, she watched in horrified fascination as one of Macon's big hands suddenly curled over the doorknob. She'd always loved his hands. Huge, slender-fingered and turned a rich copper, they were a working man's hands. "Macon," she managed to say, her pulse staggering drunkenly as he came into the dim hallway, and she stepped back to accommodate him, "I'm sure I didn't invite you in."

"Memory," he returned. "Never your strong suit."

That was rich. Didn't he recall being with Lois Potts the night he was supposed to run away with her?

"I'm coming in," he announced. "It's hot out there, Harper."

"It's Texas," she returned evenly as he stepped inside. "It's hot everywhere."

Definitely hotter in here, now that she was sharing the hallway with Macon. And yet he was right. The house was cool and dark. She'd opened the windows last night and drawn the blinds today, and even though Bruce had installed central air conditioning long ago, the house was usually cool enough without it, which was saying something in Texas. Hardly comfortable, though. With Macon crowding the hallway, she couldn't have been more tense if she were entertaining a burglar.

Not that Macon was the least bit bothered by her anxiety. Dropping his hat over the newel post, he glanced down the hallway toward the kitchen, then upstairs. When he looked through an archway into the living room, she realized how many of Bruce's belongings still filled the room. Leather-bound history volumes were alphabetized in glassed cases—although he'd worked as a pharmacist, history was his hobby—and the old-fashioned spectacles he collected were arranged on the mantel. It was an odd collection, but Bruce had possessed a questing mind, a focused intensity that allowed him to see even the knottiest problems through to the end. Sometimes, when he'd caught her lying awake late at night, Harper suspected he'd known she'd never really gotten over Macon.

"I'm sorry," she said with a start, feeling renewed determination to placate Macon so he'd leave. "I know you found those letters today. I saw you leave the post office. I...I truly don't know what possessed me to write them, Macon."

Instead of looking relieved at the confession, he pinned her with a particularly unnerving stare. "Harper," he said flatly, "I've known you for years. You always know what possesses you."

Oh, not always. She hardly wanted to examine her motives for suddenly caring so much about her appearance lately, for wearing this dress, for instance, or for pulling back her shoulder-length ash hair or spritzing her neck with perfume. "I was only doing my civic duty," she found herself admitting.

"My, my," he taunted, looking genuinely amused. "That sounds so patriotic. I'll bet the U.S. government is having a meeting right now, wishing they had a few more postmistresses like you, Harper."

"Macon," she returned hotly, unable to stand the way he was mocking her. "You can't rope in poor, unsuspecting women this way. Most women who responded to your ad need help." She exhaled an exasperated breath. "You should have read those letters!"

Tilting his head to get a better look at her, he wedged a boot heel comfortably over a stair step and raised a golden eyebrow, his voice turning silky. "You really think so?"

She nodded. "Yes, I do!"

"Hell, yes, I should have," he retorted. "They were addressed to *me!*"

Her heart pounding, she glanced around, her long-smoldering desire for Macon mixing with fury over the dire situations expressed in the letters. "There were pregnant teenagers." She defended herself. "Mothers without enough money to feed and clothe their babies, foreign women wanting citizenship because they've been separated from children in the U.S. Some are so lonely they just can't take it anymore."

His expression was infuriatingly bland, as if the catalogue of horrors didn't even touch his heartstrings. "Are *you* lonely, Harper?"

The words hit a nerve. She'd survived a teenage pregnancy and a mother who'd barely earned enough money to raise her. *And yes, damn you, Macon, I'm lonely.* Bruce had been gone two years, and Macon's unwanted presence made it seem forever since she'd been touched lovingly. Why couldn't he understand? "You can't play with people's lives like that!"

He surveyed her curiously. "Who says I'm playing?"

"I'd forgotten how impossible you are!" she snapped. No, she'd spent far too much time remembering the heat of his mouth and how his arms felt wrapped around her back. Forgetting her hair was up, she drew shaky, annoyed fingers through it, dislodging further wispy strands. "You have no concept, Macon," she continued with a soft sigh of frustration. "You've never wanted for anything, but some of those women have absolutely nowhere to go."

"Then why not let them come here?"

"Why not?" she echoed, stupefied.

His voice was a silken thread of danger. "If you hadn't written to them, they could have," he told her, his tone so reasonable she was flooded with guilt. "So, do you mind explaining why you're interfering in my love life?"

"Love life?" she repeated, the lips she'd glossed with something called Goldust Glitter parting in astonishment.

His eyes hardened. "Yes, love life."

"Since when does meeting strangers through *Texas Men* magazine constitute a love life, Macon?" Did he think she was jealous? she suddenly wondered. Even worse, *was* she? Cutting off the intrusive thoughts, she rushed on. "Macon, advertising for a bride in *Texas Men* is no joke."

He looked furious. "Am I laughing?"

"Yes!" she exploded. She leaned back against the wall and crossed her arms, the sudden drop of his heated gaze making her aware, a second too late, that the action caused her breasts to lift. "I believe you are laughing. I bet you and Ansel Walters struck a wager or something. I bet he said you wouldn't have the nerve to advertise. Why else would you do it?"

"Because I want to get married?" suggested Macon.

"Oh, please," she scoffed. "There's got to be more to it than that. You've been back in town two months, Macon, and...well, I've heard you've already slept with every available woman in town."

He had the audacity to chuckle softly. "Maybe some of the unavailable ones, too." Before she could respond, he added, "Besides, how do you know who I've been sleeping with, Harper? I don't remember seeing you in my bed."

"You have so many women you *wouldn't* remember," she returned, offering a disgusted shake of her head. "And how can you make light of this? Do you expect me to believe you're going to become monogamous just because a pregnant teenager or an illegal alien shows up on your doorstep?" Before he could answer, she shook her head adamantly. "Oh, no, I don't think so, Macon."

He squinted at her. "Why not?"

She found herself recalling his male appetite. "Because I know you."

His voice turned silky again. "You most certainly do, Harper."

Her heart was pounding too hard, and her lungs were nearly empty. If she didn't take a deep breath soon, she'd get dizzy. She forced herself to do so, gathering strength. Someone had to stop this lunacy. "To be perfectly blunt, working at the post office puts me in a position to hear all the gossip, Macon."

Unfortunately, he looked intrigued, not contrite, as if he couldn't wait to see what she'd say next. "When it comes to me, I bet it's juicy, huh?"

"I don't *ask* to hear the gossip," she said, not gracing his question with a response. "Nor am I saying any of this for your amusement." She suddenly gaped at him. "C'mon. Are you denying you and Nancy Ludell didn't leave Big Grisly's Grill until four a.m. last Saturday night? Or that you and that new teacher, Betsy, had breakfast the next morning, before you took your mother to church?" She paused, staring at him hard. "Or that you and Lois Potts didn't also go bowling in Opossum Creek?"

"Serious charges," Macon returned solemnly. "Bowling should get me the electric chair. And church...why, that should rate a lethal injection, don't you think?"

"I should be so lucky," she muttered. "Can you honestly tell me you weren't teaching an underage girl to drive a stick shift last week, and that when she drove your truck into a ditch—"

Macon's disbelieving chuckle stopped her. "Harper," he said in warning, peering at her as if she'd just stooped lower than the human eye could see, "that was Diego's *niece*."

She ignored the rush of relief. "Maybe that time," she countered. "But that's not the point. Everybody in town knows what you do, which is probably why you're trying to find a—" somehow she couldn't force herself to say bride "—woman from out of town." When Macon's jaw tensed, Harper's eyes lingered a second too long on its firm, clean-shaven line. For a second, she was sure he was considering grabbing her, and she had no idea which way she'd run—out the door or into his arms.

"Dammit, Harper." The sudden rasping curse hardly offered any comfort. "Since when are you so interested in what I do with other women, anyway?"

"I have no choice! Someone has to take an interest!" The words rang with conviction. "Don't you understand, Macon? Some of these women don't even speak English! What kind of relationship could you have with them?"

Anger had begun stoking the fire in his eyes, and now they looked lively, burning into her. "A relationship based on something other than talking?" he suggested, his tone deceptively mild.

She sighed ruefully. "I'd hoped you'd changed over the years."

"Over the years? I'm only thirty-four, Harper. Hardly over the hill."

"Your adventures around Pine Hills make that perfectly clear." Swallowing hard, she mustered her most controlled tone. "Which is why I wrote those women. Macon, the simple truth is, you're not ready to marry."

He stared at her. "That's not for you to decide."

Throwing up her hands, she glared. "You really want to make an honest woman out of someone? You want kids?" The words *honest woman* echoed in her mind, filling her once more with guilt since she'd never told him about Cordy.

"You have a problem with that?"

Damn him! Of course she had a problem with that. Was she really going to live in the same town with Macon McCann while he married one of those young, pretty women who kept answering his ads? "You're going to marry a stranger, Macon? Have a family with her?"

His smile vanished, and she had the distinct impression she'd finally gotten through to him. "You have a child," he muttered, "so you must know how fulfilling it can be."

Our child, Macon. Haven't you realized Cordy's ours? She could barely find her voice. "What you're doing doesn't even make sense," she managed to say. "You've known plenty of women, so why write to strangers? And why come back from Houston, anyway?" For years, she'd prayed he would—and prayed he wouldn't. "Everybody said you loved it there. They said you were never coming back."

He hesitated, and as sunlight shifted through a window behind him, a shadow fell, erasing the grooves around his mouth and wrinkles around his eyes, making him look so much like the boy she remembered that she could have cried.

"Cam's health isn't what it used to be."

"Oh, Macon." Instinctively, she stepped forward

and touched his arm. A heartbeat later, when his flesh gave a quick quiver beneath her fingers, she knew getting this close to him was a mistake. Seeing male awareness come into his eyes, she stepped quickly back, edging toward the wall. "Macon, I'm sorry."

"He's had a stroke already. Lost some mobility in his left arm. Now he's got to watch his blood pressure, Harper. He's got to slow down."

So do I. She was still feeling the hot touch of Macon's sun-warmed skin. "You think he'll be all right?"

"If he quits working the ranch." For a long moment, Macon was silent, his gaze trailing unabashedly to where two thin straps held up her sundress. His expression hardened. "I'm getting married, Harper," he said, his gaze returning to hers. "I'm settling down in Pine Hills, and I'm not doing it alone." Sounding gruff, he added, "I want a woman."

The raw statement of male hunger made her knees weak, and as their gazes meshed, she felt oddly disoriented. Determined to ignore the palpable energy coursing between them, she kept her voice even. "I guess I didn't want one more poor soul to get stranded in Pine Hills, the way my mama did." It was as close to an apology about writing the letters as she could get.

"You could have left, Harper." He glanced around. "Looks to me as if you did right well in this town, anyway," he mused, suddenly sounding as if she wasn't even there anymore. Finding her eyes again, he added, "Why'd you get married, anyway? It was so fast. I didn't even know you were seeing Bruce. Back then, he was...he was just a pharmacist."

Surely she was fooling herself, but she swore she

heard something that sounded distinctly like pain. She watched with astonished curiosity as Macon stepped so close that she could feel waves of heat coming from his body. Warmth seemed to push into her, and there was simply no help for how the tips of her breasts constricted, noticeably beading under the strappy dress she never should have worn. The effect wasn't lost on Macon. His voice dropped, becoming a lazy rumble, turning her bones to rubber. Her stomach muscles tightened; everything else inside fluttered.

"Why, Harper?" he repeated. "Why'd you get married?"

What did it matter to him? And why was he asking her now? Why couldn't he have stayed in Houston and left her alone? She should have said she loved Bruce, but instead, she said, "I'll tell you my motives for marrying whenever you tell me yours."

"Touché." It was only a whisper, and even if breath from the word hadn't buffeted her collarbone, the rest of him would have told her his mouth was far too close. Suddenly his thigh was lightly pressuring hers, and fingers were gliding upward on her arm, making goose bumps rise on her flesh. "Here's the deal," he murmured, sounding oddly breathless. "I came by to get a few things straight between us."

She felt faint. "I'm waiting."

His fingers tensed on her arm, almost hurting. "You never waited, Harper."

Her temper flaring, she stepped back, then realized she was pressed against the wall. Her hands skated behind her, flattening against the plaster for support.

"Save the fancy verbal moves for your bride. You're the one who left Pine Hills."

"But I'm back." Macon's eyes captured hers, holding on so fiercely she didn't think he'd ever let go. "This might be a small town, but it'll have to be big enough for us both. From now on, leave my mail alone, and I'll forget about the letters and not press charges."

She swallowed around the unexpected lump forming in her throat. "Thanks for letting me off the hook."

"No problem." He drew a deep breath, and she sensed he was affected by the scent of perfume he took with it. "I know you planned to leave here years ago," he said, seemingly trying to hide how affected he was by her proximity, "but you married Bruce, and now things haven't turned out the way you wanted, so you're meddling in my life. You're mad because I left here and lived my dreams, Harper. But I forgive you."

So that's what he thought. Pain sliced through her at his lack of understanding. She had no idea where her mama's dreams ended and her own began. Her mother had hated Pine Hills and wanted Harper to leave. *Escape*, she'd called it. But Harper had liked doing her homework in the Laundromat after school, listening to the familiar rhythmic sound of the dryers while she joked with customers. She'd liked sneaking off to meet Macon, too. She knew she was smarter than average, but she'd never needed to be somebody important. Her voice caught. "Maybe there were other dreams, Macon." *Like leaving town with you.* She could hear her mama's voice. *You think that rancher's boy cares about you, girl? No, ma'am. He's the richest boy in town. To him, you're just some girl that's gonna wind up working in a*

Laundromat like your mama. For a breathless moment, dread pushed at Harper's chest, and she thought she'd suffocate.

"Harper?"

All the air left her lungs. "I'm sorry for what I did, Macon," she said, knowing she had to make him leave. "Really. Please, you'd better go now."

He become utterly still. Only his breath moved, teasing her ears as he leaned nearer. "What if I don't want to?"

Gazing at him, she suddenly couldn't pull her eyes from his mouth. A kiss would mean so little to him, she thought illogically, craving a taste. According to gossip, he dispensed those kisses all the time. He let them fall from his damnable lips like spring rain. Maybe if she had just a taste of him, she could finally forget him.

His voice was mesmerizing. "What if I want to stay?"

"You always did do exactly what you wanted, didn't you, Macon McCann?"

"Then I sure as hell shouldn't stop now," he drawled roughly, brushing his body against hers, the taut, hard sweep of his hips coming with a rustle of denim. She hadn't looked down, hadn't known he was aroused, but she felt it now. He felt so hard and hot and thick that her knees nearly buckled.

"Where's Cordy?" he said.

Hearing her son's name brought her to her senses, but Macon had already filled the space between them. How could she fight what she felt right now? She couldn't bear to admit it, but she'd probably lured Macon here by writing those letters. The seductive dress, upswept hair and new makeup were telling, too. A heartbeat passed, then his throaty words slurred against her hair. "Where?"

She could feel his lips brushing the strands. Her heart beat wildly. *Get away,* she ordered herself. *Sidestep. Brush past. Push open screen door. Step outside and breathe deeply. Clear your head, Harper.* It should have been so simple, but the eyes riveted to her lips were all amber fire.

"Where, Harper?"

She shouldn't have said it, but she did. "Not here."

Hot was the first thought that came a second later, when Macon's mouth crushed down on hers. *Burning hot.* Moving with unrestrained trembling hunger, he parted her lips with the slow thrust of his tongue. Wrapping his arms tightly around her waist, he steadied her as he kicked the storm door, shutting out the summer sunlight. He threw the dead bolt, the loud click making her pulse soar, the masterful strokes of his tongue making her climb. Up through dark tunnels, she strained for the feeling, whimpering and aching as practiced, work-roughened hands deftly slid between their bodies, caressing her breasts and belly as they swiftly unbuttoned the front of her dress.

She reached down, her fisted hand opening on a hard-muscled thigh before sliding over to grasp him intimately. He was so aroused, so big, all throbbing ready heat pulsing through denim. Her dress was open, too—all the way now! Just as she squeezed him firmly, her fist closing around his length, he pushed the dress from her shoulders, making her head swim as he exposed her bra.

She couldn't believe what this man did to her, no more than she could understand why she hadn't felt this with Bruce. And then those thoughts were gone because Macon was admiring her with a hot gaze, looking down, his greedy eyes devouring her belly and simple white panties. He brushed his knuckles over the mound, lightly grasping her tangled hairs through the silk, then quickly, he unhooked the front clasp of the bra and pushed the cups back toward her shoulders. The way he looked at her bare, aroused breasts made her feel heartbreakingly beautiful. His whisper was hoarse, the words slurred. "I've missed this, Harper."

Sucking a breath through gritted teeth, he used both hands, lifting and cupping her breasts from beneath, mercilessly kneading them, pushing them high and pressing them together, deepening the damp crevice between them as he locked his groaning, liquid mouth to one. Releasing a throaty growl that, alone, was enough to make her shatter, he ground himself against her, rolling his hips as she arched to meet him. She cried out, gasping as he bit, nibbled and soothed a painfully erect nipple with his mouth, leaving her so damp between the legs that she was shaking. Only after long, torturous moments did Macon lean back, tersely demanding, "Look at me, Harper."

She did, and the past vanished. There was only their present connection—light and shadow playing on his face, the warmth of long-suppressed desire in his eyes and finally the blessed fusion of his searing mouth to the breast he'd already left glistening. Thrusting her fingers into his hair, she whimpered again, twisting for the rasp of his teeth. Chest heaving, she drew in the woodsy scent of him, everything inside her reaching higher, endlessly higher like a kite, as his urgent hand tugged down her panties.

"There, Harper," he soothed, in a ragged whisper, his hand parting her knees, and then gentle thumbs pressing circles ever higher on her open thighs. When he reached the apex and stroked the pearl he'd laid bare, she was so lost she barely even heard the rake of his zipper, but she plummeted into a whirlpool of wet, blind darkness when his bulging thighs pressured hers again. She'd waited so long for this...for him. Dizzy, her knees weak, she clung to his shoulders. Lower down, she felt the hair that protected him, rough and tangled and wild, and then the raw living silk of his erection. She'd never known a man could get so hard. The dangerous thickness of the shape made her gasp, and he moaned his response, dragging his trembling lips back and forth across hers. "Harper...oh, Harper."

Darkness was still pooling in her thoughtless mind when his first hard, swift thrust lifted her. Lights flickered and went out, but she was climbing, her head flung back, her hands curling over powerful muscles, her fingers digging into work-honed shoulders, tightening with each new furious onslaught of scalding kisses that prepared her for the fall. Against her cheek, his words were rough, torn sandpaper. "I didn't... won't..."

Her mind was spinning. *Come inside me? An old promise. Oh, God, what am I doing?*

But she wanted this, she had for years. Heaven help her, but after Bruce died it was sometimes Macon she'd imagine, his body loving hers until she didn't feel so alone. Suddenly, she was tumbling downward, spinning, her body shaking, the pulling depth of her shuddering climax making her mind blank again as she convulsed.

And then, just like that, he was gone. A wrenching gasp was torn from him. Another as she felt the warm gush of his release as he withdrew. The loss was so abrupt, so jarring, that her heart seemed to go with him. Stunned, strangely bereft, she wondered how this could have happened.

Macon had come about those letters, and the next thing she knew...

She steadied herself, her hands flying to her bra and dress, gathering the sides. She pulled up her panties so fast they wedged in her behind, and by the time her shaking fingers were through buttoning, he was buckling his belt. Even worse, the damn man was grinning. "Are we still here, Harper?"

Didn't he know she felt like her dress—like she'd come apart at the seams? That she was still throbbing, her heart still racing out of control? Didn't he understand what he'd just done to her?

Judging by his grin, she guessed he did. "I don't know how that happened," she whispered.

His breathing heavy, he eyed her a long moment, and by degrees, his grin vanished and his jaw set. "I thought things might be different now."

Different from what, Macon? Different from when I came to tell you I was pregnant—and found you in your truck with Lois Potts? Different from when you went to Houston without me? A lump formed in her throat. "Different?"

"I thought...maybe with Bruce gone, and Cordy almost grown. And given the fact that Cordy and I are on good terms..."

Everything inside her seized up. "Good terms?"

He stared at her. "He does work for me, you know."

She didn't. Her heart missed a beat. "At the ranch?"

Macon frowned, his hand resting on the belt he'd just buckled. "He didn't tell you I hired him to work Saturdays?"

No! She thought he came home dirty on Saturdays because of summer football practice. Why had Cordy gone behind her back? He had a generous allowance, a car, and he'd promised to concentrate on his studies this summer. The shock, on top of what had just happened between her and Macon, was too much. Realizing she'd buttoned her dress crookedly, she tugged it down, trying to smooth it, but Macon had wrinkled it beyond repair.

He was already opening the storm door, glancing through the screen as if he wanted to be anywhere in the world but in a dark hallway with her. "I guess you figure I'll destroy your son the way I would any woman I marry," Macon said, not bothering to hide his temper. "But don't worry, Harper, I'll tell Cordy that the Rock 'n' Roll won't be needing him anymore." Macon shrugged. "Guess you don't know everything about your son."

She wished something, anything, would stop the too-fast beating of her heart. "You don't, either, Macon," she whispered miserably.

Lifting his hat from the newel post, Macon put it on and adjusted the brim. "Good to see you, Harper."

Given what had just happened between them, the words seemed the worst kind of understatement. Her lips felt swollen. Tendrils of hair were glued to her neck with perspiration. She crossed her arms over the cockeyed dress, feeling ridiculous. "That's all you're going to say about what we just did?"

Macon shot her a level glance. "What do you want, Harper? A blow-by-blow analysis? A report?"

"No," she said, coloring, "but—"

"If I think of anything to say, I'll send you a postcard," he assured dryly. "Somehow, I'll bet you're one of the people around this town who still gets her own mail." Turning, Macon pushed through the screen, casually walking across the porch and into the sunshine. When he was halfway across the yard, he lifted the hat, waving it once as a parting taunt sounded over his shoulder. "I mean it. *Real* good to see you, Harper."

She glared at his back, her eyes narrowing. Mustering her gamest tone, she offered her own sugary Texas drawl. "So glad to oblige, Macon."

A throaty chuckle floated back.

Pressing her fingertips to the wire mesh, she stared at him through the screen, shaking her head. She'd repay him for this. She didn't know how yet, but she'd think of something. And when Cordy got home, they were going to have a serious talk about his working on the ranch. For now, she simply watched Macon. Just as when he arrived, he was circling the lilac, forsythia and snowball bushes, then he got into his truck and slammed the door.

Torn apart by mixed emotions, she whispered, "It's like watching a rewinding movie." Except a lot had happened between the past and the present, and during Macon's short but rather eventful visit. As he'd ambled through her yard, his open shirttails had blown in the breeze as if to announce to the neighborhood that he'd recently had little use for clothes. And as he backed his truck from under the willow, he had the nerve to toot his horn as if to say he'd definitely be back for some more of the same.

Staring at the last glimpse of his red truck winking through the trees, Harper softly, solemnly vowed, "Never again, Macon McCann. I mean it this time. Never again."

3

HARPER HAD LED HIM ON and rejected him for the last time, Macon vowed as he galloped toward the ranch office. She should have been hog-tied for meeting him at the door wearing that sinful sundress dotted with dusky bluebonnets the color of her eyes, the heavy, milk-satin breasts Macon remembered all too well straining the straps. Glancing at the new fence as he flew past, Macon added, "Guess it'll hold."

Harper's dress sure hadn't. He barely noticed the nearly full moon, or the orange and purple clouds bracketing a bloodred sun that was taking a final peek as it dipped behind rolling green hills. He was still seeing shadows slanting on her skin and thrusting his fingers into pale hair he'd left disheveled around her shoulders. He was still considering that deceptive blond-haired, blue-eyed, little-girl-next-door facade that always fooled him until he looked closer and noticed broody eyes that were too aware and a mouth that was too sassy because of her repressed need for kissing.

At least Macon had kept his cool when he left, but now he couldn't believe his lack of willpower. How could he stop himself when her body tucked so perfectly into his, though? When the soft smoothness of her skin glided under his mouth like water? And when her incoherent whimpers cooed around his ears, begging him to burrow into wanting heat? Cursing soundly, Macon fought memories of the burning relief he'd felt as he entered her....

But she didn't trust him.

If she'd wanted a relationship, she'd never have written those women or looked so distressed when she realized he employed Cordy to do odd jobs. She wouldn't have berated Macon for dating—something he'd only done to save face with her!—or implied he was some kind of latter-day Don Juan, which he wasn't. Truth was, Harper wanted sex. *He* was the one who'd always wanted more. Love. Companionship. Marriage. Babies.

But not now.

Never with her. Judging from her readiness, she'd been just as long without good loving as Macon, perhaps since Bruce's passing. Macon realized that, with Bruce gone, he could admit how envious he'd felt, looking at that farmhouse. Everything hurt—from Cordy's sandbox to the petunia boxes to the leather-bound books so neatly arranged in cases in the living room. The construction company Macon had started in Houston ran itself now, but so far, it was all there was to the Macon McCann legacy.

Macon wanted a family house, though, on the west meadow of the Rock 'n' Roll. He wanted cute kids, who'd ask the same things he used to ask Cam. *Do cows bite? Why can't I eat grass, if cows can? If a cow pie's not really a pie like an apple pie, then why do we call it a pie?* If Macon didn't act soon, he'd be the last of the McCann line. Cam's ribbing aside, he knew his folks were anxious for him to settle down.

Which meant he had to let go of Harper for good.

Dismounting at the office, Macon set the gelding loose, then went inside, seated himself at the desk and shuffled through the women's letters. No pictures were attached. No doubt, if there were any, Harper had thrown them away, not that it mattered. A woman's looks weren't important, just her personality. That was exactly where Harper was lacking.

As he carefully read the letters from the respondents to his ad, he found what Harper said he would—stories of war, tragically ended love affairs and separated families, some written in languages Macon didn't recognize, others badly worded by translators. Frustrated, he chewed his lip, asking Harper's question. How could he get to know a woman who didn't speak English? He'd picked up enough Spanish to get by in Tijuana, but that was about it.

"You've got to find *somebody*," Macon muttered. "For Cam's sake," he added, his resolve strengthening as his traitorous mind recalled Harper's thighs opening like rippling water, then remembered the swing on the wraparound porch from which she and Bruce must have watched the world go by. His chest constricted. *She'd* had companionship for years, and now *she* had a growing, active boy, and memories of a husband to keep her warm at night.

What did *he* have?

Nothing. Only the hope that marrying another woman would get the silken feel of Harper off his hands. He mulled over the women in town again. Lois

Potts and Nancy Ludell were divorced and looking, and then there was Betsy, the schoolteacher from Idaho. None seemed right, so he picked out the only five letters written in good English. They were from a seventeen-year-old girl named Chantal Morris, a thirty-year-old hairdresser who worked on movie sets in L.A. and who'd never visited a ranch but wanted "to do *City Slickers* meets *Baby Boom.*" Macon wasn't up on movie lingo, but he rented videos, so he supposed that meant the woman wanted him to get her pregnant on a ranch, which, at the moment, was fine by him. Between the lines, he could tell Anna Gonzales wanted citizenship. A New York divorcee named Judith Stone complained she was bored since her kids had left the nest. She also worked in a battered women's shelter and politely informed Macon that she wouldn't give out her age until they were married for years. Finally "a simple, earthy, country gal" named Carrie Dawn Bledscoe wrote from West Virginia, saying she was desperate to get hitched to a cowboy.

The command of English aside, something in each letter touched Macon, either with pity or laughter, and he genuinely wanted to help. Scrounging in a drawer until he found a pen and paper, he began to write.

Dear Chantal,

Sounds like you're in a bind over there in Missouri, so I'm sending you a ticket to Pine Hills, Texas. Because I got so many responses to my ad in *Texas Men*, I'm inviting five finalists to the ranch. I figure this will take some pressure off us all while we're getting acquainted. There's plenty of room at the ranch house—you girls can

bunk down together—and I'll be planning a
week of fun-filled activities to introduce you to
my family and ranch life. Rest assured, we'll all
have a great time, regardless of the outcome.
However, as I said in my ad, I'm very seriously
marriage-minded. So, by the end of the week, I'll
have arranged for a reverend....

"YOU'RE WHAT?" Cordy Moody was pacing around the
ranch office like a caged animal, and when he angrily
tugged off a straw hat, shaggy ash hair fell into smoky
blue eyes that Macon suddenly wished weren't quite
so much like his mama's. They blazed at Macon.
"You're *firing* me?"

"That's not exactly how I'd put it, Cordy—"

"You can't!"

Macon winced, hating what he was doing. Personally, he thought Cordy needed this job. He was finding
men to look up to, and he'd filled out physically. Macon guessed his good looks and athletic build were
bringing him his share of the girls already. Hard to believe Macon had been that young when he'd met
Cordy's mother. "Sorry," he forced himself to say,
knowing he'd miss seeing the boy with whom he felt
he'd forged a relationship, "but I don't have a choice. I
talked to your mama last night, Cordy."

Talk hardly covered what had transpired, and in the
short pause when Macon took a deep breath to process
that, Cordy interjected, "I don't believe this!"

Macon didn't, either. This morning, still ruled by his
temper, he'd driven to the Opossum Creek post office
where, without incident, he figured he could express

mail the letters he'd written last night. As soon as he reached the ranch, he'd called in Cordy, not about to let Harper think he'd continue employing her son against her wishes.

Cordy grunted, the angular face that kept Harper from being model pretty giving him a harder, masculine edge, despite his age. "Let me guess," he growled. "She's mad because I didn't tell her I was working. Well, why would I? She would have said no."

Macon frowned. "I thought you two got along."

Cordy shrugged. "I guess, but she won't let me get a job. She's overprotective, even though my grades are good. They were all As this year, except for history."

Maybe that's why Harper didn't want him to work these few hours a week. History had been a hobby of Bruce's. Every summer when he was alive, Bruce had organized the annual civil war battle reenactments at the county fair in Opossum Creek. "You failed history?"

Cordy glared at Macon. "I got a B. Why doesn't anybody trust me? My mom needs to get a life. She hasn't gone on a date—" the tough, adolescent posturing dropped "—since Dad died."

Hardly wanting to hear about Harper's dating practices, Macon shoved his hands in his jeans pockets, lifted his boots and crossed them on the desk. "Well, Cordy, I'm sure your mother'll—" the words stuck in his throat, his mind filling with the many shattering things Harper could do "—date eventually."

Cordy didn't look convinced. "No, she won't. She's too busy recording my every move. She's suffocating me."

Macon could imagine. She sure as hell hadn't thought twice about opening and answering Macon's mail. "Mothers are like that, Cordy. But she loves you."

"Too much." Cordy flung himself into a chair, his face darkening. "And now you're on her side," he accused. "She told you to fire me, didn't she? She probably *paid* you to fire me. She doesn't want me mad at her, so she's making you do her dirty work."

"I'm not *firing* you, Cordy." Feeling strangely roped in, Macon added against his better judgment, "Maybe I can talk to her." He'd meant to avoid Harper, at least until his female guests arrived, but Cordy wanted to work, and it wasn't his fault he'd come to the Rock 'n' Roll. How was he to know Macon and Harper had a history? One as recent as yesterday, Macon thought, wincing. Still, working was good for a boy who lacked male influence. "Maybe she'll let you work somewhere else. Maybe down at Happy Licks, or the bowling alley over in Opossum Creek."

"I work *here!*"

Cordy was usually such a reasonable kid. "It's just a ranch," Macon reminded him, unable to fathom why he was taking this so hard.

"No, it's not."

Caught between a rock and a hard place, Macon chewed his lip. Regardless of Macon's personal feelings, Harper was the boy's mother. On the other hand, he didn't want Cordy thinking he wasn't valued. Choosing his words carefully, Macon continued, "Your mother and I go back a ways." *All the way back to fourteen hours ago.* "And she's...well, she's not real comfortable with you and I having a relationship. We went to high school together, and I think she's—" Macon searched his mind "—worried about my reputation around town."

Cordy gaped disbelievingly. "She doesn't want me here because you've got all those girlfriends? What's wrong with a guy having a few girlfriends?"

"Maybe she believes more goes on than really does," Macon said diplomatically, fighting awareness of what *had* gone on. "She just doesn't feel this is the best environment...."

"Environment?" Cordy looked stupefied. "I'm harnessing cattle so Diego can give them shots! Last week I mucked stalls. Even when you weren't around, I worked over here, you can ask Cam. I've been doing this for two years, Macon."

"And lying to your mother about where you go on Saturdays." When Cordy flushed guiltily, Macon said, "Look, her not wanting you here is due to issues that...I can't go into." Now, there was an understatement. "But it's got nothing to do with you."

Cordy glared at him. "You are *so* wrong. I know why she's mad. It's because Bruce wasn't my dad."

Macon squinted, anger curling through him. "What nonsense has someone put into your head?"

"That someone was my dad. *He* said he's not my dad. I mean, he's my dad because he raised me and all, and even though he died, he always will be. But it was another man who got her..."

"Pregnant?" Macon couldn't believe this. "Who?"

Cordy rolled his eyes as if unable to believe Macon's stupidity. "You."

"SLOW DOWN, MACON!" Clutching his hat and the dashboard, Cordy said, "If you think Mom's mad about me working for you, how do you think she'll feel if you wreck and get me killed?"

He was barreling down a five-mile gauntlet of furrowed flatlands planted with cabbage that lay between the McCann ranch and the Moodys' and, realizing the boy was right, Macon pulled off the road and put the truck into Park, deciding he'd better just sit a minute. He'd already heard everything Cordy had to say, how the boy had become suspicious over the years because of overheard whisperings between Harper and Bruce and because of how nervous his folks acted when Macon came into town. Now everything inside Macon was shaking, and his hands felt as if they were trembling even though they looked perfectly steady on the steering wheel.

Peering at him and looking uncomfortable, Cordy lifted off his straw hat, rested it on his knee and toyed with the brim. "Maybe I shouldn't have told you, Macon."

"Yes, you should have." His heart aching, Macon looked abruptly through the windshield, staring blindly into a blazing morning sun that promised another scorcher. He and Harper had a child? Cordy was his? *Why didn't you tell me, Harper? How could you deny me a life with my own son?* Knowing Cordy was watching him, Macon pretended to swallow his anger. Cordy was already confused enough, and Macon would do anything he could to make things work out all right. No wonder Harper hadn't wanted him around Cordy.

She'd feared something—a gesture or word—would alert Macon to the truth.

Still looking anxious, Cordy traced a thumb back and forth over the hat brim, his nail grating against the straw. After a moment, he stopped and fiddled with the heater vent. "Maybe we shouldn't tell her we know, Macon."

Macon turned to Cordy, his eyes roving over the boy, his throat constricting. Not confront her? His voice came out coarse, roughened by emotion. "You're sure about this?" God help the boy if he'd concocted this story for some mysterious reason only another teenager might understand.

Cordy glanced away, and Macon pretended not to notice he was fighting tears, since Cordy didn't like sharing his emotions any more than Macon had at that age. When he turned to Macon again, his chin had quit quivering. Macon couldn't help but study the boy's face, although he was still unable to see anything of himself in Cordy; he was so much Harper's boy, with ash hair and blue eyes.

"I'm not lying, Macon," Cordy continued, slicking his palms worriedly down the legs of his work-soiled jeans. "Dad said Mom would never tell me, and Gramps and Gran Moody died not knowing, so he figured I had a right to know before he died." Cordy's voice shook, and once more Macon graciously pretended not to notice. "I guess...I guess you've got a right to know now, too, Macon."

At least Bruce Moody had instilled some wholesome, honest values in Cordy. Macon's heart thudded dully. His voice was almost a whisper. "I can't believe you've known this for *two years*. Since your dad..." As he said the word, the truth hit home again. *He* was Cordy's dad, also. "Since he died?"

Cordy nodded. "The only person I told was Garrick, since he's my best friend. I would have told you before, but you were in Houston. And then, a couple of weeks ago, I stopped in to see Mom in the post office, and Betsy—you know, the new art teacher you went out with?—well, she told Mom you'd come back to work the Rock 'n' Roll. That's when I realized you'd be staying this time." Cordy squinted, his eyes—so like Harper's—knitting with concern, looking wiser than their years, the eyes of a boy who'd lost a father. "And then last Saturday," Cordy continued, "Diego told me Cam won't let you run the ranch until you get married. Is that true, Macon?"

So, the Pine Hills gossip machine was still well-oiled, Macon thought. *Just wait until everybody gets hold of this latest news.* And they *would* get hold of it. Macon wasn't sure what he was going to do, but he was sure of one thing. He intended for Cordy to inherit the Rock 'n' Roll. *If he's really my son.* His heart stretched, almost hurting as his eyes drifted over Cordy. "Yeah," he managed to say, "it's true. Cam wants me to get married."

Cordy took a deep breath. "Well, when I found out you were back for good, I figured I'd tell you, but..."

He hadn't known how. Suddenly, Macon realized the boy—his son—had been hanging around the Rock 'n' Roll for two years, hoping to run into him and tell him the truth. In two years, he hadn't, though. That hurt more than anything else. Didn't Cordy know he could tell Macon anything? Barely able to find his voice, Macon said, "You did the right thing."

He nodded. "My dad was a great guy. I miss him."

Macon calmly said, "Of course you do. He's your father. He always will be." He couldn't have Cordy thinking Macon would try to replace him. Probably Harper had been carrying his child, Macon supposed, but she'd wanted to marry Bruce. It was that simple. She'd known Macon would propose if he knew she was pregnant, and she didn't want it known around Pine Hills that she'd turned down the natural father of her baby. Taking a deep breath, Macon tried not to think of how he'd missed Cordy's childhood, of how many times he'd spoken with Cordy without knowing their real relationship. How would their conversations have been different? He wasn't sure, but one thing he knew: he never wanted to see Harper again. He would, though, only for Cordy's sake. His fingers tightened over the steering wheel, and finally he said the only words worth saying. "I'm sorry about all this, Cordy."

They were the only two people for miles, surrounded by rock bluffs, rolling farmland and the cabbage furrows. When Cordy raised his gaze, it held wisdom beyond his years, and something hushed came over the truck. "Don't be sorry for me, Macon. I did okay. I'm sorrier for you right now."

Truer words had never been spoken. Cordy had always had a family, but Harper had robbed Macon of his for years.

ONE LOOK at Macon told Harper something was terribly wrong. "Cordy?" she called.

He brushed past her, heading straight upstairs, his gangly strides taking the steps two at a time. As she whirled toward Macon for explanation, his stunned expression almost made her forget that yesterday, just inches from where they stood, they'd made love. Almost.

"Was there an accident?" she demanded, dread filling her. "Who was hurt? What happened?" At least Macon and Cordy were safe! Trying to keep the panic from her voice, her hand closed on a white terry robe draped over the newel post. "Cordy?" she called, squinting upstairs, her heart racing with fear. "Can you come back down here, please?"

She *knew* she should have called Cordy home from his sleepover last night to tell him he was no longer allowed to work at the McCann ranch. What on earth had happened this morning? Obviously something so bad that Macon, of all people, had brought Cordy home. Where was Cordy's car?

As her eyes searched Macon's, she suddenly realized she wasn't dressed. Despite the staffing problems at the post office, she was off this morning and Cordy was gone, so she'd pampered herself with a long bath. A red shortie gown clung to her damp skin, and she grabbed the towel wrapped around her head, unrolling it so that it draped her shoulders, covering her breasts. She reached for the robe again. "Just let me put this on, Macon." When he grabbed her wrist, she gasped. "What are you doing?"

Despite the angry heat of his gaze, her heart beat wildly, and she caught her lower lip with her teeth, biting hard, as if that might stop the thoroughly unwanted, involuntary impulse that made her nipples bead. "Please," she whispered indignantly, "just let me have my robe."

His voice was gruff. "It's nothing I haven't seen before."

And touched and kissed. Heaven help her, it wasn't, Harper admitted, her knees and jaw slackening as she reached willfully past Macon and swirled the nubby robe around her, knotting it. "Now, what are you looking at?"

"Like I said, nothing I haven't seen a thousand times before."

"My son's here," she hissed.

"*Our* son."

The whole world seemed to stop. He knew! Somehow, he'd found out! So that was why he looked so furious. Realizing her worst nightmares had just come true—and only hours after she'd so foolishly made love with Macon—Harper took a step back, but his fingers circled her wrist and hauled her closer. She froze, knowing she couldn't afford to get emotional. Maybe she'd heard wrong. It was a long shot, but she ventured, "What are you talking about?"

In the cool, dim hallway, the usual amber of Macon's narrowed eyes darkened, turning the color of toasted, buttered almonds. "You know what I'm talking about."

Her gaze darted to the stairs. "Keep your voice down."

"Cordy's the one who told me. He told me because I've moved back to town with every intention of staying."

Impossible! She grabbed at the wall for support. "Cordy told you?"

"Bruce had some integrity. He told Cordy before he died."

Her throat closed with emotion, her ears against a truth she couldn't accept. "Cordy's known..." A shaking hand covered her mouth, and worried eyes flashed toward the stairs. "No," she whispered through her fingers. "Cordy would have told me he knew." She tried to wrench her wrist from Macon's grasp so she could run to Cordy, but Macon held fast. How could Cordy have known? And for all this time? Her son told her everything, didn't he? Wouldn't she have guessed? "I was going to tell you the night we were supposed to leave town together." She defended herself.

Macon's voice was strangely cold. "You never even met me."

Torn between her desire to go to Cordy and to explain to Macon, she managed, "Mama caught me trying to leave the house, so I was late, that's all." Anger equaling his threaded through her words. "I found you down at Big Grisly's Grill with Lois, and the next week you were in Houston."

He frowned, his hand loosening, but only for a heartbeat. "Lois Potts?" Before she could answer, he said, "And Bruce just stepped into your life then? How long had you been seeing him, Harper?"

Her heart pulled. When she'd gone to the brand-new pharmacy in Opossum Creek, hoping to escape prying eyes in Pine Hills while she bought a second home pregnancy test, she hadn't realized Bruce was the owner. For years, his family's pharmacy had been situated next to the Laundromat her mama managed, and he'd decided to expand the family's business with a second shop. After he'd sold her the test, she'd wound up telling him everything, and he'd responded with more compassion than she'd ever known. Now, because so many important things depended on what she said, she managed to soften her voice. "He said he'd fallen for me over the years. He gave us a good home, Macon."

Macon surveyed her just long enough that she felt the pressure of his thumb on the frantic pulse of her wrist, just long enough that she felt searing heat seeping through his jeans, just long enough that she wanted to be anywhere but here with him.

"A good home. Obviously, I couldn't have provided that."

"Not when you were in Houston!" Swiftly, she grasped an edge of the towel that was around her shoulders and dabbed at the dampness on her face from her wet hair. "Oh, maybe you could have, Macon," she said. "I don't know." Sixteen years ago, her mind was reeling with the damning, inflammatory talk her mama had used to control her and keep her away from boys. Talk that it had taken Bruce years to get through. Her voice broke. "It was a long time ago."

"Maybe," Macon said, eyeing her as if he hated her. "But I read those letters you wrote just yesterday, so obviously not much has changed. You still don't think I deserve a woman. A marriage. A child."

Contrary emotions were tearing her apart. She feared losing Cordy, and maybe even Macon, she didn't know. "Deserve a woman?" she found herself retorting hotly. "Didn't you have one yesterday? Heaven knows," she added under her breath, "you probably had another one last night, too."

He looked as if he could have her again—right here, right now. Despite the circumstances, his steady gaze made her too aware of being bare-legged and damp, of how her nightie was clinging. Edging closer, his thigh sweeping hers, she felt she'd just brushed up against everything she'd ever wanted.

"That I did," he agreed roughly.

Her tone was insistent, hushed. "Cordy's here. Let me get my clothes so we can sit down and have a decent discussion."

Macon's drawl was thick, heavy as molasses, his eyes burning. "With you, I never seem to want decent, Harper."

"You need to hear my side of this, Macon," she said, keeping calm. "So does Cordy."

Macon's sharp eyes were cutting her like diamonds. "I've had sixteen years of your side of things. Now you're going to hear mine. Earlier today, Cordy accused you of being meddlesome. He said you wouldn't even let him get a summer job. He feels like he's suffocating. And you know what? I defended you, but the fact is, I'm suffocating, too. You've made decisions for me for the last time. I had every right to know this."

It was true. She knew it. But Macon hadn't loved her, and Bruce had. And yet, decisions she'd made years ago suddenly didn't seem so clear. Still, wasn't it right to raise your child with a man who loved you?

"Sixteen years," Macon muttered, "and here you are, still ruining my life."

The conversation was taking a new turn. "What?"

"I'm talking about those letters you wrote!" Macon growled, dark, smoldering emotion filling his eyes, then helplessness. He lowered his voice. "What do you have against me?"

"*Nothing!* I set you free to pursue your life," she said, her voice insistent. "If your folks found out I was pregnant with your baby, they'd have forced you to marry me. You'd have felt trapped. You had dreams, Macon. You wanted your own business." Guilt crowded in on her. What if she was wrong? What if he'd have *willingly* married her?

When he said nothing, she assured herself her mother had been right about him. Besides, Harper had seen Macon and Lois with her own eyes. Even if Harper had married him, she'd have doubted his fidelity all her life. She'd have become one of those distrusting wives who second-guessed their husband's every move. Whenever he was late, she'd have stood by dark windows, staring from curtains to driveway, looking for his truck, wondering where he was and who he was with.

His voice was strangely calm. "Why did you write them?"

Because I can't stand to see you marry somebody else. Quickly suppressing the truth, Harper parted her lips to speak and realized Cordy was on the stairs. "Honey?" she whispered.

"I'm okay, Mom." With the additional height of the steps, he looked so tall, so close to grown up and so like Macon, with that strong jaw and naturally bemused curl to his mouth. Leaning to one side, he shouldered a duffel, and the sudden surge of her blood took her breath. "Where are you going?"

"To live with my father."

Deep down, maybe Harper had known this would happen someday. Nothing ever stayed a secret in Pine Hills. Late at night, alone with her fears, she'd lived this moment a thousand times. She'd been a good mother. She'd opened lines of communication, talked over all the issues with Cordy—school violence, safe sex and drugs. She'd done everything she could to make his life perfect, even married a man she loved, but not passionately.

Now she had to let go. Otherwise she'd be everything Macon claimed, meddlesome and controlling. *But it hurts so much to see him leave with Macon!* "All right," she forced herself to say as Cordy came downstairs. "But not before we talk about this."

"Mom." Her son's eyes met hers. Thousands, maybe millions of times, she'd gazed into those fog-blue eyes so like her own, but now Cordy seemed far away, like a distant stranger. "Just once, let me do this my way. Dad explained things. And I'm not mad. Dad agreed with what you did, at least when you did it. And I've had a long time to think about it. But now I want..."

To get to know my other father. The only saving grace was that Cordy hadn't packed enough clothes to last a week. Still, she could barely breathe. "Okay." What else could she say?

Cordy glanced at Macon. "I'll wait in the truck."

Macon stared after him, shocked. "Harper," he said, once Cordy was gone, "I don't even have a room set up."

If her heart wasn't breaking, she might have actually laughed at Macon's statement of unpreparedness, but her emotions were engaged for Cordy's sake. "He wants to get to know you." *And damn you, Macon, don't deny him the chance.*

Macon eyed her. Clearly, there was much more to be said, but he settled on saying, "Let's get one thing straight, Harper. I won't be used in a battle between the two of you, and I'd like to have him, but..." Pausing, Macon grunted in frustration. "Right now, I've got five women coming to town."

Ten minutes ago, she'd have thought nothing more could have unsettled her. "Five *what?*"

His eyes hardened. "You didn't mail letters to everybody, you know. There were still some unanswered letters to the *Texas Men* ad. So last night, I invited five women to spend time on the ranch."

Last night? After they'd made love? Harper's eyes widened in hurt surprise. "Women?" she repeated idiotically. "What *kind* of women, Macon?"

"You know," Macon returned gruffly. "Women."

She was stunned enough to say it out loud. "After what happened here?"

Because of it, his eyes seemed to say. "Look, Harper, Cam's sick, and he'll only turn over the ranch to me if I'm married. He's had a stroke that's ruined his hand, but he keeps driving cattle anyway. Next time he might not survive."

"I'm sorry."

"I don't want pity."

Somehow, she was sure Macon would stop Cam before he went too far and destroyed his health. "I should have known." She managed to speak despite her shock. "Ever since last night, I've been flooded with guilt. When you said you wanted a wife and kids, do you know what that did to me, Macon? Last night, I almost believed you really wanted to get married and have babies. I realized I'd had no right to withhold the truth about Cordy from you. I'd taken something precious." After he'd gone, she'd curled up in bed, crying, doubting every secret she'd ever kept.

After glancing toward the truck, Macon turned back to her. "Glad to see you've got a conscience," he said, then took another tack. "Those letters...were moving. There was something real in them." The drawl that did such crazy things to her insides turned terse. "Something *honest*, Harper."

Swallowing hard, she stared through the screen at their son, her equilibrium starting to return. Cordy loved her. Things would work out between them. And this was so like Bruce. For a second, she felt as if he'd touched her from the grave. She thought of how she and Cordy raced to the hospital after hearing the news of the interstate pileup that had left Bruce critically injured, and of the time Cordy had spent alone with his father. As he'd been dying, Bruce wanted to give his son another father.

"Honest," she echoed, lifting her eyes to Macon's. "Marrying for something other than love isn't honest." She wished she hadn't said it. Cordy was the issue right now, not her marriage to Bruce or Macon's to a stranger.

"Cam won't slow down, and it's going to kill him," Macon returned. "In a roundabout way, my marriage is going to save his life, so I guess you could say I *am* marrying for love."

She took a deep breath. Years of imagining this horrible scenario where Macon confronted her had prepared her to deal with him. "I've worked hard to raise a good boy, Macon. Church every Sunday. Good grades. Community service."

"Worked hard? Or controlled his every move?"

Her jaw was set. "I've worked hard to instill good values." Scarcely able to analyze what was driving her, she added, "Among them, that people marry for love." Bruce hadn't stolen her heart as Macon had, but she'd loved him. "Cordy's about to learn that's not always true." She raised a staying hand and rushed on, willing herself to be strong. "Which is fine. I understand the pressures forcing you to marry, Macon. But given how things stand now, I have concerns."

He stared as if he couldn't believe her nerve. "Concerns?"

"This woman's going to become Cordy's stepmother."

Macon's jaw slackened. "I hadn't thought of that."

Before she knew what was happening, a speech even Harper couldn't believe was rolling off her tongue. "Well, I have. I'm a mother, and mothers have to think of such things. Since you're only doing this for Cam, not because you're in love, then you shouldn't mind my input at all. Like it or not, this woman—this *stranger*—is going to influence Cordy for years to come. Call me controlling or any other name you choose, but it's only fair that I interview these women. I *have* to," Harper emphasized. "I haven't worked this hard at raising Cordy only to see some...some person I don't even know twist his head around."

Macon seemed to be recalling how twisted Harper's own mother could be—that gave her reason for worry—but the slight widening of his eyes also made his shock apparent. "You want to meet these women?"

"I feel I should be involved in the..." Harper simply couldn't bring herself to say *wedding*, not that she believed Macon could really go through with this. "In the process," she finished.

Macon's gaze held anger and wary distrust, uncertainty when he glanced toward the truck, then curiosity when he looked at Harper again. Curiosity seemed to win. "Okay, Harper. You can have some input."

4

PINE HILLS welcomes Macon's brides!

Macon's eyes trailed slowly over the bold type on an artfully composed flyer Lois Potts was holding as she stepped through the post office door onto the blistering sidewalk beside him. At least the gossip mill hadn't gotten hold of the fact that Cordy was his son. "Yet," Macon muttered under his breath.

"No wonder you're talking to yourself, Macon," Lois chided, looking somewhat hurt by the announcement Harper had taken the liberty of distributing all over town. "You must have loads on your mind."

Macon was thinking of Cordy and Harper. "More than I can say, Lois."

"Well, I simply can't believe you're doing this!"

He wasn't. Feeling torn between fury and a twinge of amusement that surprised him, Macon glanced below the boldly printed headline to where Harper had reproduced his *Texas Men* advertisement, offered short biographies of the five visiting women and invited the community to various events where they could welcome them, including a hayride, poolside barbecue, nature hike and dance that was to be held in the McCanns' barn. Given that he'd just found out about Cordy, Macon had expected Harper to lay low. But no. In large print at the bottom, Harper had boldly written,

"Lifeguards still needed for the splashy pool party!" Shaking his head, he wondered why she was trying to antagonize him and make him look like a fool.

Lois was anxiously finger combing her dark blond jaw-length perm, and as Macon glanced over her, he recalled the night he was supposed to leave town with Harper. After she stood him up, he'd wound up at Big Grisly's Grill, and he'd come close to hitting the sheets with Lois. He hadn't, though. While he wondered what Harper had seen, he hadn't had the nerve to ask.

Now, looking at Lois, he felt something akin to pity. She'd been a young beauty who'd gotten too much, too soon in life, and now she was stinging from a divorce and caring for four little ones alone, and her usual perkiness seemed forced. Actually, Macon thought the hard knocks had made her more compassionate, which was why he'd asked her on some casual dates when he'd come back to town. That, and to keep his mind off Harper.

"Harper's done such a great job," Lois said with a trace of hurt that made Macon's eyes narrow. Her character might have softened, but Lois had never disguised the fact that she'd wanted Macon. Even back in high school, she'd been jealous whenever she'd seen Macon with other girls. "Everybody in town's talking about your upcoming nuptials, Macon."

"Well, we *do* have Harper to thank for the advertisement," Macon agreed. She'd left flyers on bulletin boards, countertops and under every windshield wiper in Pine Hills. Mostly, Macon hoped, the flyers were now in the front seat of his truck, since he'd been busy collecting them all morning.

"And Harper says the women'll be here tomorrow," continued Lois in disbelief. "So, you're definitely getting married on the following Saturday?" Before he could respond, she rushed on. "Yesterday, when I stopped in the post office, Harper said she'd beat you to the punch and talked Reverend Shute into canceling a fishing trip so you—and whomever you decide to marry—can go straight to the chapel after your blood tests. Harper said you'd written the women, saying you'd have a reverend ready when they got here, and now everything's arranged."

Macon managed an easy smile but was still wondering what Harper was up to. After what he'd just found out about Cordy, he wouldn't put anything past the woman.

"I'd never have the nerve to do something such as this, Macon, but with four kids, I could sure use a husband," continued Lois with a shaky, self-conscious laugh. "I just want you to know you've got my support. Marrying a woman you don't know seems strange, but everyone in town wants to see it work out. We'll help any way we can."

"What would I do without you?" Macon asked dryly.

Lois looked as if she wanted to say something more, then changed her mind. "Inviting all of Pine Hills to help welcome your future bride is so sweet, Macon. I..." She paused, eyeing him a long moment. "I never knew you had it in you."

"Look, Lois, I didn't really—"

"It's like something out of a romantic movie," she added. "And if it works, I might place an ad myself. I almost answered a personal ad once, then lost my nerve. But yesterday, I said to myself, 'Lois, if a man like Macon can come right out and admit to everybody in Pine Hills that he hasn't been so lucky with women...'"

Macon nearly choked. "Lois—"

She shook her head, not about to be interrupted. "What you've done takes real courage, Macon," she continued, holding up a staying hand. "Most men couldn't—"

"Lois, I'm not—"

Cutting himself off, Macon blew out a sigh. He felt trapped. Once more, Harper had caught him between a rock and a hard place. He couldn't explain the whole situation to Lois, but if Macon had known he'd be sharing his home with his son—a son he'd never even known about—he definitely wouldn't have invited five females to visit. Muttering a vague excuse about needing stamps, then saying an appropriate goodbye, Macon held open the post office door and glared toward Harper's work station.

"It figures," he said. No Harper. A temporary worker, probably from the Opossum Creek post office, was behind the counter, sorting letters into bins. Turning, Macon watched Lois cross South Dallas Street and nearly collide with Harper, who was exiting Happy Licks Ice Cream, cone in hand. "So, there you are." Macon headed around the corner of the post office to the parking lot, keeping his gaze locked on Harper, feeling like a hunter with the prey firmly in his sights.

Crossing his arms, he leaned against the driver's side door of his truck to wait for her, the sticky heat doing absolutely nothing to improve his mood. Since Cordy had moved to the ranch three days ago, Macon hadn't yet seen her. Now, as he watched her, Macon wished he could end their relationship, but knew he never could now, because of Cordy.

After a moment, Macon quit fighting the heat. After tossing his hat into the front seat, he stripped off a sweat-damp T-shirt and threw it next to the hat. Leaving the door open so air could circulate, he rested his bare back against the hot vinyl edge of the seat cushion. Harper finally crossed the street, the very picture of summer innocence, her tongue delicately lapping the top of the cone, strands of fine ash hair blowing across her cheeks. How could someone who'd lied for years look so sweet? Suddenly furious, Macon thought of how he'd run into her, Cordy and Bruce around town in the past—at the Feed and Seed or Happy Licks or over in Opossum Creek at the bowling alley. To her credit, he guessed, Harper had tried to avoid him, but when that was impossible, she'd smiled and made small talk. How was her deception even possible, when she'd known Cordy belonged to Macon? What was going through her mind? Didn't she feel any guilt?

"I'll never know," he muttered. Today she was wearing the navy slacks to her postal uniform, and the red-white-and-blue string tie she was required to wear hung loosely around the unbuttoned collar of a white blouse. He was half tempted to strangle her with the tie. Macon guessed she'd left her jacket inside. She was so busy—intent on pushing dark sunglasses up on her nose, licking the cone and looking both ways for traffic—that she didn't even notice Macon until she was halfway across the parking lot.

She stopped like a deer caught in headlights.

Instinctively, he flashed an unconcerned smile, telling himself he didn't care about her negative reaction to seeing him. *He* didn't intend to be impolite. *He* had no reason to be defensive. She was the one at fault. In fact, maybe he'd even further imbalance her, throwing her off guard with his kindness and charm. It was exactly the sort of response she deserved, given all she'd done. Deciding that, he broadened his grin.

The ploy must have worked because Harper didn't move. She was gauging the situation, and Macon could name the exact, panicked moment when she realized there was no escape. She had to pass him to get to work. Looking resigned, she squared her shoulders and started walking. When she was within earshot, he said, "Now, aren't you the picture of innocence?"

"If you want to talk about pictures, Macon," she drawled, stopping in front of him, "I guess we could start with that beefcake photo you sent to *Texas Men.*"

He couldn't see her eyes through the dark lenses of round, wire-rim sunglasses, but he could swear he felt the heat of the gaze studying his bare chest. He sighed. "The day you're innocent, Harper—"

"I'll let you know, Macon," she assured him, her smile benevolent. "You might want to mark it on your calendar."

"A red letter day to be sure," he returned.

She lifted an eyebrow, her tone wavering precariously somewhere between wary distance and mild flirtation. "Speaking of personal presentation, since you're downtown, maybe you should put on some clothes."

Registering her annoying determination not to acknowledge how she'd wronged him, he returned the volley. "My bare chest distracts you? No shirt, no shoes, no service, huh?"

"Everybody knows men who want service in Pine Hills—" Harper jerked her head toward the hills, in the direction of a place called Rosie's "—generally head that way."

"I wouldn't know."

Her eyes narrowed in disbelief. "You've never been to Rosie's?"

Once more, he cursed the impression that he was a man about town. By creating it, he'd only hurt his own reputation. "If I had been to Rosie's, I guess I could tell you." He flashed a smile. "After all, you've proven how well you keep secrets."

That remark stopped conversation cold.

She blushed. "Please. Don't start with me, Macon."

"I haven't even told you why I'm here."

"Not yet." She ventured a slow, tentative smile. "But you will. Just don't get mad. For Cordy's sake, we need to be civil to each other right now. I wasn't attacking you."

"No?" But she was convinced he was a playboy. Despite her continual rejection, it seemed he could still arouse her jealousy, something he didn't quite understand. To test the theory, his low, unconcerned drawl floated on a wave of afternoon heat. "Anyway, Lois didn't seem to mind my bare chest."

"Sheriff Brown might arrest you for indecent exposure."

"Better than mail fraud," he retorted. Harper didn't exactly have the right to play the heavy. "Your cone," he added.

Suddenly realizing the hundred-degree heat was doing a number on her ice cream, Harper started, looking flustered. She quickly licked the cone, catching pink dribbles. "Anything particular bring you to the post office today?" she inquired between licks, obviously trying to regain her emotional balance. "The new Marilyn Monroe stamps? Jiffy bags?" Her voice caught. "Cordy? Is he okay? Is that why you're here?"

"He's just fine, Harper. And you know why I'm here."

She glanced away, suddenly looking so lonely and vulnerable that, unbidden, Macon's heart did a three-sixty in his chest. Around town, Harper was well-respected. She was the kind of woman who took chicken soup and slippers to neighbors when they were in the hospital over in Opossum Creek, and while she did gossip in the post office, just as she had in the Laundromat when she was a teenager, she was motivated by a genuine love for people.

Only when it came to Macon did she start acting strange. Right now, she looked worried sick about Cordy. The sunglasses, Macon realized, probably hid dark circles under her eyes. "Trouble sleeping?"

"Some," she admitted with a sigh. "Why are you here?"

As Macon dug in his back pocket, his eyes lowered, landing on her blouse. The white cotton had wilted in the heat and shouldn't have been sexy, but Harper was obviously unaware an extra button had come unfastened, exposing the lace edge of her bra. His groin swelling, Macon gritted his teeth and tore his gaze from where it had settled on a tantalizing hint of a breast. He pulled the flyer from his back pocket, unfolded and held it up against his bare chest. He still had plenty to say about Cordy, but for the moment, it seemed better to stick to simpler issues. "Seems you've been doing a lot of writing on my behalf lately, Harper."

"The flyer? You don't like it?"

"Dammit, Harper!" he exploded. "These are everywhere."

"Not everywhere," she assured him, the quick, mischievous twist of her lips giving him no comfort whatsoever. "I still have a stack to deliver to Big Grisly's Grill, though I did manage to slip the flyers, folded and stapled, into the Sunday bulletins at Christ's Church."

Macon tried not to react. "In the *what?*"

Her widening smile shouldn't have been nearly so appealing. "The Sunday bulletin."

"Harper," he said, her name a warning.

Again, that innocent smile. "So much for gratitude, Macon," she chided. "You were baptized there, and it *is* where you're getting married next week, so it seemed reasonable that the congregation would want to share in all your joy."

"I admit," Macon said on a sigh, "I was curious when you insisted on becoming involved in my choice of a bride, but this..." He didn't have words to describe how he felt. "Couldn't you at least *act* contrite under the circumstances?"

A guilty flush stained her cheeks, but she forged on, clearly driven by some perverse motive he couldn't begin to fathom. "You wanted to get married as soon as possible, because of Cam's health? Isn't that what you said?"

"I thought you, of all people, believed in keeping matters of the heart private." He couldn't help responding dryly, "After all, you kept secrets to yourself for sixteen years."

She ignored the barb, though he was satisfied to hear the heightened pitch of her voice, which indicated her emotions were running high. "Your marriage is a matter of the heart now, Macon?"

He'd finally gotten to her. Good. "Maybe not," he admitted, "but I wouldn't have involved everybody in Pine Hills." He surveyed her a long moment, then couldn't resist pricking another nerve. "If I didn't know better," he continued, "I'd think you were jealous and trying to make me look like a fool."

"Now, *that's* a bit dramatic."

He didn't think so. No woman made love the way she had four days ago without feeling something for a man. But jealousy in the wake of her rejection stung. Even though they shared a son, she'd never wanted anything more than sex with Macon. He pried his eyes from where she was wiggling her tongue against the ice cream, then tried not to notice when she moved closer, into a wedge of shade cast by the open truck door.

"It's hot," she murmured in explanation.

And always hotter whenever Harper was around. "Sure is."

When she finally spoke again, the sudden soft catch in her voice affected Macon's emotions more than he wanted to notice. "Look," she said, "I don't want to argue. How's Cordy?"

"Settled in at the ranch."

"Settled in?" Harper bit down, her straight white teeth tugging her lip. "So, he's fine? Are you sure? I started to call. I *wanted* to call, but..."

"You need the number?" Even after all these years, Macon still remembered her mama's.

Color rose on her cheeks. "No...uh, I remember your phone number, Macon." She lowered her voice, and once more something soft as velvet touched the words. "Do you remember how, back in high school, we'd turn down the ringers on the phones, so our folks wouldn't hear, and call each other in the middle of the night and talk until dawn?"

Of course he did, and he damned her for calling up the memories. "Yeah. But what I really want to know is how, in all those hours of conversation, you failed to mention a pregnancy?"

She swallowed hard. "I told you how."

As if he'd believe she was motivated by self-sacrifice. Did she really expect him to believe she'd married so Macon could go to Houston and start his construction company? Suddenly, Macon didn't feel quite so convivial or willing to discuss Cordy. Truth was, becoming a father and son sixteen years after the fact was unnatural, and his and Cordy's previous relationship, contrary to what Macon had hoped, wasn't helping.

For the first two days, Macon had tried too hard, rustling up activities he and Cordy could share—until Cordy blew up, saying Macon was as intrusive as his mother.

"Has Cordy...said anything about coming home?"

Macon stared at her. "I figure he *is* home, Harper."

Her voice trembled. "Oh, dammit, I guess that's true."

Macon stared at his boots, then at a white spot of sun on the pavement, and when his eyes returned to the impenetrable lenses of Harper's sunglasses, he told himself once more to stick to the simple things first and discuss the flyer, and yet he couldn't. "All those years..." Macon dragged a hand through his hair and shook his head. If Harper had really come to meet him, why hadn't she? Was it because he'd been with Lois? He wanted to ask but couldn't bring himself to.

"Macon." Her voice fluttered, just as her blouse collar did in the summer breeze. "Please. Let's not talk about it. We'll just wind up mad. It was a long time ago."

He didn't care if it was yesterday, but she was right. They had a teenager to worry about now. Macon wasn't prepared for the quick toss of Harper's head or the sudden challenge that came into her eyes. "Okay," she amended. "I take it back. I'll ask you once. If you'd known I was pregnant, would you have married me, Macon?"

She'd touched a nerve. He wasn't about to grace that with a response. "You've kept your secrets, so maybe I'd like to keep some of mine. And anyway, it doesn't matter, does it? You decided for me, Harper. I'd already asked you to run away with me."

"I didn't need to run away. I needed to face my life."

A life, he thought, that rightfully should have included him. Macon bit back a curse. Just looking at Harper reminded him of her hallway...of how easily his hand had glided down the tiny white buttons of her dress. Was it really only four days ago? Maybe, he thought. But memories of loving her had been haunting him for years, and it wasn't fair that the recollections stole his anger every time he deserved to be mad. What if he'd never learned the truth? What if he'd never found out he had a chance at fatherhood—a chance some men never got?

"Cordy called me yesterday, just to say hi," she finally said. "He said you told him to call. Is that true?"

Nodding grimly, Macon wished Cordy had kept that gem to himself. Macon hardly wanted Harper knowing how much he considered her feelings. Still, he figured she was lying awake every night, just as he was, mulling things over. "Yeah. I told him to call."

"Thanks," she said on a rush of relief that brought Macon more pleasure than he'd admit to. "I've been so worried. Oh, Macon, I can't believe he never told me he knew—"

"Tread lightly, because you're walking on eggshells, Harper."

"Eggshells?"

"Yeah. I can't believe *I* never knew."

At least she had the decency to blush. Behind the dark glasses, he couldn't see her eyes, and yet he could swear they'd drifted to his chest again. The gaze—

whether real or imagined—warmed him, making him aware of her as a woman. For a long moment, he watched in silence as she attacked the ice cream—this time seemingly to squelch anxiety. Wrapping her tongue around the base, she stroked the sides, making the melting ice cream look so good that Macon almost felt it sliding, freezing, down his own throat. All at once, the searing metal of the truck seemed too hot, too close to his bare skin, seeping through his jeans to his backside and eliciting a slow, pulling sensation in his loins. Oblivious, Harper licked her lips nervously. "Are you *sure* Cordy doesn't need anything from the house, Macon? Clothes or something?"

Macon tried to remind himself she hardly deserved his pity. "No, he's fine. And to be blunt, I don't like being in the position to reassure you."

She stiffened. "I'm sorry. I'm just..."

"Worried. I know. But if he wasn't doing fine, I'd tell you."

She studied him a minute, her voice hitching with tentative surprise. "You know, I think you would, Macon."

He'd never lied, so such a tentative expression of faith in him grated. "Of course I would. *I'm* honest, Harper, unlike some people we know. Anyway, I didn't come to talk about Cordy today. I think we should each think this situation through, not say anything we'll regret. We both want a relationship with him, which means we have to get along."

"I agree. I appreciate your being—"

"Nice under the circumstances?" Macon was, but if she applied just one more nervous, quick, upward thrust of her tongue to that damn ice cream, he'd lose his mind. Against his will, he found himself saying on another sigh, "Cherry or raspberry?"

For a second, she stared at him blankly, her pink pointed tongue flicking at the corners of her mouth, then she glanced down and wrapped a paper napkin around what was left of the cone. "Uh...raspberry," she said warily, as if she hardly trusted the new direction of the conversation.

Macon leaned, his hand covering hers just long enough to register the feel of her skin—all creamy, smooth heat—as he took the cone. "Not my favorite, but it'll do."

She cracked an anxious smile. "What's your favorite?"

"DQ. Double soft serve. Chocolate dip." He wondered what she was making of this exchange. Was she slowly circling the issues for the same reasons he was? Did she want to try to be friends? If so, for Cordy's sake or her own? He wished he knew his own motives, but every time he got around Harper, he felt confused.

Her glance was dubious. "If it's not your favorite flavor, then why not leave me the rest of my lunch?"

"Ice cream for lunch? Very unhealthy."

She arched an eyebrow. "Shouldn't you be busy branding cattle or something?"

"Not when I can be stealing a girl's lunch."

"No problem. I never eat in front of friends unless there's plenty to go around."

He considered, his heart rate accelerating in a way he chose to ignore. "Are we friends, Harper?"

She shrugged. "Sounds dangerous."

Definitely dangerous. Especially since their history insured they'd never be friends. Sun was baking the concrete, and Macon could still feel her eyes on his chest as he dipped his head and licked her cone again. Feeling the sweet, cold ice cream slide down his throat was no less a shock to his system than tracing his tongue where Harper's had been. He could swear he tasted her, not the raspberries, and the mere idea made unwanted desire pool in his lower abdomen. He settled a palm on the warm taut skin of his belly to steady himself as he handed back the cone.

"Thanks, Macon."

"Have the rest."

The air-conditioning inside the post office would have been preferable to the sultry parking lot, but neither moved, and Macon found himself admitting that just living in the same town set his mind running on the Harper track. Even before he knew the truth about Cordy, she'd kept crowding into his thoughts.

"What are you thinking, Macon?"

That she was pretty, standing there with her eyes hidden and sunlight shining through her hair. He shrugged. He knew they needed to talk, but he wasn't sure how to start. Handling relationships was a woman's job, right? In books and movies, men were the barbarians. The guy worked hard, played hard and brought home the bacon until a good woman finally took pity and turned him into a tolerable human being. Women were supposed to be angels. Not so Harper.

Which was why, if Macon had the sense God gave a horse, he'd get in his truck and leave right now. "After I told my folks about Cordy," he began, "my mother went over to your place, and then she came back not three hours later. She didn't offer a word of explanation, but now you two are thick as thieves. What's going on, Harper? What did you say to her?" Without letting her respond, he muttered, "Next thing I know, this flyer's all over town."

He shook his head. Harper might have kept their grandchild from them, but Cam and Blanche had rebounded within moments, almost as if they'd guessed the truth all along. They knew Harper from the post office, and now Blanche was getting to know Cordy while planning both Macon's wedding and Cam's retirement. Ever since Cam's stroke, she'd been desperate to have Cam turn the ranch over to Macon. Now, with Harper's help, Blanche had apparently phoned the *Texas Men* respondents. Macon had arranged for their flights, but she'd coordinated rides from the airport. Last night, while Macon and Cordy were out fishing, Blanche had started fixing up the room the women would occupy.

Even though Harper made his mouth water in weather that could parch an ocean, he realized he needed to keep his distance. God only knew what she'd do next. He watched as she parted her kissable lips and crunched nervously into the cone. "Harper, when I said you could meet these women, I didn't mean you could cozy up to my folks or take over my life."

"Macon," she countered without the slightest trace of irony, "did you really think you could write a few letters and wind up married within a week? These things take planning."

"So, you and my mother decided I needed some help?"

"That sums it up."

"My mother doesn't even think I'll really go through with this, Harper. She's hoping Cam'll back down and let me start running the ranch. I wrote those women because I wanted to *meet* them, not necessarily marry them in a week."

Harper shook her head. "No, Chantal was kind enough to read me her letter over the phone. You said you'd pick a bride by the end of the week, and we just want to make sure you can. Since you hadn't taken care of it yet, we arranged for blood tests and for Reverend Shute to be in town. Your ducks are all in a row."

Shute, he thought. Right about now, it seemed an apt name for a preacher. Aloud, he said, "If my ducks are in a row, I guess I could use a rifle."

Harper laughed, the airy sound just bothersome enough to elicit emotions Macon had vowed he'd ignore. Despite his mood, he felt the sudden urge to smooth back her blowing hair. Without even moving, he could feel the strands falling through his fingers, softer than velvet ribbons. Vaguely, he wondered how things would have turned out if it had been him, not Bruce, pacing at the hospital in a paper gown, waiting to be handed his newborn. Macon wondered where he was when Cordy was born. Attending night classes he'd taken in Houston, maybe, or charging around a construction site.

Harper gingerly proffered the remaining bite of the cone. "Care for the rest, Macon?"

The rest? A knot of concealed temper uncoiled. *I*

wanted it all, Harper. Maybe he wouldn't have been a good father, but he'd deserved a chance. Emotion made his voice drop, deepening it, turning it husky. "Sure," he forced himself to say, taking the cone. "Why not?" *There're a thousand reasons why not.*

Glancing past him, she was staring inside the truck, taking in the flyers he'd collected from all over town. She flashed another fleeting smile, as if determined to smooth things over for Cordy's sake. "Already got cold feet, Macon?"

Was it his imagination or did she really sound hopeful that he wouldn't go through with it? Was Harper toying with him, thinking she'd call his bluff and maybe prove he wasn't the marrying kind? Or was she just jealous in a way she couldn't admit to herself? Macon glanced toward the dusty brown, sun-baked hills in the distance. "Cold feet?" he murmured. "Not in this weather."

"They say it's a hundred and three in the shade."

She'd edged further into the shadowy darkness near the truck door, so close he could have pulled her into his arms without even moving. Good thing he didn't want to, he told himself.

Looking uncomfortable at the lapse in conversation, she added, "We could use some rain."

Were they really standing out here, exchanging pleasantries? he suddenly wondered, feeling another rush of resentment. Given the secrets she'd kept, Macon shouldn't even be speaking to her. If he'd known Cordy was his son, he'd never have mailed those letters. He wanted to spend time with his son. Should he retract his offer to the women? Or quickly marry, force

Cam into retirement and then focus on getting to know Cordy?

Harper had grown quiet and watchful.

"Like my mother, you don't believe I'll really get married, do you, Harper?" he asked. "That's it. You think you're going to call my bluff."

"That's not the same thing as taking over your life, is it?"

She'd taken over his life the first time he'd laid eyes on her. "Sure feels like it."

Now she looked more sure of herself, and she smiled. "You'd best get used to women having their way with you. Wives require attention, and whichever woman you marry will have a say in all your decisions from now on."

"I doubt I'll feel the pinch. She'll be family."

"And soon."

Was Harper really arranging his marriage to another woman?

"You've got to admit," she continued, as if reading his thoughts, "this is going to get interesting, Macon."

"Oh, Harper." He was unable to keep the seductive edge from his voice. "It already *is* interesting."

She sucked in an audible breath. "If by interesting you're referring to what happened in the hallway the other day..."

Vaguely, he wondered how the conversation had dovetailed back to that. "Unfortunately, I'm remembering every detail."

"We'd better both forget it."

So, she was remembering, too. Knowing better, but

unable to stop himself, he swiftly leaned and caught her wrist. "What if I can't forget?"

"Forget it anyway, Macon." Her words lacked conviction.

His fingers locked more tightly around her wrist, the quickening beat of her pulse making his heart race. "I have," he reassured huskily, drawing her deeper into the cool shadows behind the truck door, his throaty drawl dipping to a whisper. "I've forgotten how I unbuttoned your dress." She was close enough that he could see her eyes widen behind the dark lenses of her glasses. "And how my teeth felt, rasping against your breasts. I forgot how you wrapped your legs around me, and your arms..."

Her lips pursed, but despite the schoolmarmish set of her mouth, he could tell she wanted him. "I don't find you nearly as irresistible as you seem to think, Macon."

"I'll never forgive you," he murmured, unable to withhold the admission as he gazed at her, "but I'll never stop wanting you, either, Harper." It was probably the wrong time to imagine his mouth covering hers with sudden savage vengeance. He knew exactly how she'd feel crushed against him, and just thinking about it made him hard. For a brief second, in his mind's eye, he was gliding a hand upward, his fingers circling her delicate neck as he deepened a kiss. Her mouth would be as hot as the Texas sun, her breasts as full as summer fruit, and her body would flow against his like water. She would taste of cool, sweet raspberries.

The soft, inviting way those pursed lips suddenly parted didn't help matters. "Macon?"

"Forget it," he managed to say gruffly, his gaze still riveted to her tempting mouth, his fingers uncurling from around her wrist. "Don't worry, I'm not going to kiss you, Harper."

She whipped off her glasses, then stared studiously at the lenses, scrutinizing them as if they'd broken during a kiss they'd both only imagined. "Of course you're not," she said levelly, without meeting his gaze. "You're getting married next week."

"True." Knowing he couldn't stay here even a second longer, he suddenly hopped into the truck and stared down from the cab, still wanting that kiss. It would have been as deep as Star Point Lake and just as wet.

She'd have kissed him back, too. But then, just as in her hallway, Harper would have backed away, and Macon had too much pride to live through that again. Slamming the truck door, he said a quick goodbye, then turned the key in the ignition and pulled away.

She shouted, "I'll be at the ranch tomorrow, when the women arrive. When Cordy called, I told him to expect me."

Was Harper really going to insist on interviewing these women? Sighing with frustration, Macon cleared the parking lot, but a wry smile suddenly twisted the corners of his mouth when he glanced in the rearview mirror. The good widow was still standing in the parking lot, gaping at his taillights.

Watching her, he could almost forget what she'd withheld from him over the years. Almost. Maybe anybody who made a U.S. postal uniform look so appealing deserved forgiveness. He actually considered throwing the truck into reverse and going back to fetch her.

However, his slight smile vanished when he reached the end of South Dallas and glanced up. Braking the truck, he found himself staring at a banner above the street that said, "Pine Hills Welcomes Macon's Brides!" Macon took a deep breath. "You'd better watch out, Harper," he warned softly, "or it's you I'll take to that altar."

5

EVERYBODY AGREED that Macon's brides were the most interesting thing to hit Pine Hills since the Star Point Lake froze over in the winter of 1992. Only talk of Cordy's being Macon's son, information Cordy himself let drop in aisle four of Potts Feed and Seed, overshadowed it.

The news of Cordy's paternity spread like wildfire, but Cordy seemed to take the gossip and questions in stride. Harper wasn't nearly as comfortable with the whispers around the post office, but was otherwise glad to see Cordy acting like his usual self. He'd rebuffed her attempts to speak in depth about the past when she arrived at the ranch this evening, saying he was busy driving his potential future stepmoms from the airport.

Now Harper leaned back in an armchair, tugging down the knee-length hem of a mint-green sundress with a sweetheart neckline. They'd just spoken with a woman named Judith Stone and were waiting for the next woman to appear. "Loosen up, Macon," Harper forced herself to say. "These poor women are here to meet their future husband, not the Grim Reaper."

His lips quirked in a bemused smile, making clear he wasn't going to let her slow, mocking drawl rile him. "No black cloak," he said, looking more at ease with her than he had in years as he pushed from the doorway where he'd been lounging. "No scythe. No white horse."

Glancing over his jeans and short-sleeved yellow button-down shirt, Harper frowned, wishing he didn't look quite so good. "Death rides a white horse? I thought it was black."

"Maybe I'm confusing myself with the knight in shining armor."

She chuckled dryly. "Oh, that's you, Macon."

His words were mild. "There was a time you thought so."

Wishing Macon would quit saying such inflammatory things, Harper glanced around the study while searching for a retort. In the north wing of the ranch house, this room was cozy, with tall, gleaming windows and polished wood floors, all of which kept reminding her she'd once secretly dreamed of living here with Macon. "Well," she finally said, shooting him a long look, "if I don't see a black cloak, I guess I don't see a suit of armor, either."

"I'm still shopping."

"Where does a cowboy go for a suit of armor these days?"

"Sam's Club. They have everything."

Before she could stop herself, she laughed, but sobered just as quickly, recalling the steely light of determination that had come into Macon's eyes yesterday when he'd left her in the post office parking lot. "Careful, Macon," she warned, watching him, "or you'll wind up getting married as a point of pride."

"You really think I'd lose the bachelorhood you're

sure is so important to me just to save face in front of everybody in town?"

"I'm sure of it."

Pausing in the middle of the room, he stared at her. "Get this straight, Harper. You might think I'm not serious about this, but I don't care what other people think. One of these women is going to be right for me, you'll see."

Did he really think so? Or was he baiting her? Harper's heart missed a beat, and she was still trying to ignore what felt suspiciously like panic when Macon strode toward her armchair and stopped beside it. Staring up, she met his gaze. It was direct and penetrating, full of fire and knowing promise. Why was he unsettling her like this? Just to prove he could? Or because flirting with her meant nothing now, since he really intended to marry another woman? "Okay," she murmured. "I admit it, Macon. I want to see how far you'll go before you turn tail and run from the altar."

He was towering above her, the strength in his body imposing, his husky drawl a near whisper. "And if I don't run?"

"You will," Harper assured him. His eyes narrowed, and once more she noticed lines that hadn't been there years ago, and how time, or the sun, had turned his golden hair even lighter, more like sunlit wheat than honey.

"You're dying to get me out of the way, aren't you?" he asked mildly.

She edged back in the armchair, snuggling into the cool leather and staring at him as if she'd never heard anything so ludicrous. "Why would I want you out of the way?"

"Because you won't feel safe until there's a ring on my finger," he said, his low chuckle seeming to curl into her blood. "And another woman in my bed."

"Why would that make me safe?"

As if just to taunt her, Macon seated himself on the edge of the armchair and glided a finger along her cheek. "Because then I'll be off-limits, Harper."

"I'm hardly chasing you, Macon."

"For someone not chasing, you sure catch me a lot."

True, and somehow she supposed it was as inevitable as the return of summer. "Since I doubt you'll be faithful, your wearing a wedding ring wouldn't make any difference, anyway."

His sudden chuckle broke the tension. She watched the crow's feet around his eyes deepen with the deliciously rich sound. "I won't be faithful, huh? How do you know? Are you planning to keep tempting me once I'm married?"

It would be easy enough, she admitted to herself, her eyes dropping over the broad chest straining his pressed shirt. "Of course not. I don't fool around."

His voice was all silky challenge. "You don't?"

She thought of her hallway. "Not usually." She corrected herself. "But sometimes I meet with obstacles."

He chuckled. "Let me guess. Bramble bushes? Deep rivers? A behind full of cacti?"

"Men," Harper clarified, relieved to hear a rustle from the hallway. Seemingly realizing how close they were, Macon stood abruptly, almost guiltily, and she flushed as his thigh brushed her shoulder. What was wrong with her? she wondered. They were here to meet his potential brides, but she and Macon had been flirting, pure and simple.

"Hello there," said a tall Mexican woman, stepping into the room and seating herself directly in front of Macon, her sparkling dark eyes looking so curious that Harper's hackles rose. "I'm Anna Gonzales."

Her voice was like butter, and she was beautiful. Harper tried to fight it, but her face fell, and she felt a knife stab of jealousy. Ignoring her discomfort, Macon made small talk, leaving Harper to dwell on Anna's startling physical attributes, not the least of which was the waist-long blue-black hair that hung in waves down her back. She was a south-of-the-border Scarlett O'Hara, feisty and vibrant with poreless rose-tinged skin, large breasts and an impossibly narrow waist.

Somehow, Harper managed a smile when she was gone. "Well, you have to admit—" she couldn't help but prod, trying not to sound too interested in his re- action "—Judith Stone was much more mature." Har- per swallowed hard. "And Judith wasn't nearly as old as you expected, Macon." Mustering further enthusi- asm for Judith, Harper's voice suddenly shook. "Judith was really nice."

Macon scrutinized her a long moment. "Anna's younger," he argued.

In that instant, she felt sure he was going to marry Anna Gonzales. "But Judith's not that much older than me, Macon."

"You're not in the running, Harper."

Feeling flustered, she swatted him, but he leaned lithely, catching her hand and trapping it against his thigh. Fighting breathlessness, Harper inhaled deeply, but that only brought to her attention his scent of soap and pine. "But maybe you're right, Harper," he suddenly continued, dropping her hand and frowning as if seriously considering Judith, who'd been pleasantly, not unattractively plump, with riotous, curly short black hair and blue eyes as vibrant as Liz Taylor's. "Judith's a young forty," Macon agreed. "Mature. And she sounds fun. I liked her immediately, and I've got nothing against marrying an older woman. Besides, I already have children, as it turns out."

"Child," Harper couldn't help but whisper.

Despite the fury she knew he still harbored toward her, lights danced in his golden eyes. "Anyway, you know what they say about older women."

"No," she returned with an annoyance she couldn't mask. "And, frankly, Macon, I don't want to. I just wish the next woman would get here."

Macon didn't seem to hear her. "Judith's lonely now that her kids have moved out."

She was smart, too, and quick-tongued; she'd run a home for battered women in New York City for years, but when her husband left her, she decided she needed a change.

"*Mashana macomb, mashana mazel*," she'd said with a sophisticated smile, the depth of character apparent in her bright blue knowing eyes. "It's a Yiddish expression that means if you change your place, you change your luck." She'd glanced around the study, looking delighted. "Of course, I never imagined I'd become a rancher's wife." Offering Macon an inviting smile Harper had no right to find so deeply disturbing, Judith had stared at Macon with those heart-stopping Liz Taylor eyes and unabashedly said, "Until now."

Harper wished she'd never forced the issue. Maybe none of these women would have come to town. Lost in thought, she barely heard the knock at the door, but when she glanced up, she saw a young woman with short red hair bounce into the room. She was wearing faded jeans and a green-and-white checkered blouse. "Hi!" she said in an accent so twangy that Harper could barely follow. "I'm Carrie Dawn. I'm from West Virginia. And see, I've been working at the Mountaineer Equipment Company for two years, ever since I got out of secretarial school. We're a franchise for heavy equipment, bulldozers and tower cranes, you know?"

"You don't say?" asked Macon, sounding genuinely interested, and for the next few minutes, while Harper stewed, the two chattered amiably about heavy equipment Harper had never even heard of.

"Anyway," Carrie Dawn continued, apparently tiring of the topic of bucket excavators and rotary blast drills, "I know secretaries shouldn't get involved with their bosses." She chuckled knowingly. "Kisses around the office mean you can kiss your sweet career goodbye!" Pausing, she slapped a hand to her jeans-clad knee for emphasis. "But my boss, Charlie, and I've been dating on the sly for two years now, ever since I started with the company. So, right before my two-week vacation this year, I said, 'Charlie, it's my way or the highway. Marriage or nothing.'"

Carrie Dawn's brisk voice suddenly wavered. "But then, Charlie never called me. So, I never went back to work after the vacation, and now I'm out of a job. Yesterday, I sent him a letter with your *Texas Men* ad, Macon, saying I'm going to marry you." When she smiled bravely, myriad freckles jumped around on her face. "I hope that's okay."

Macon shifted uncomfortably. "But it sounds like you're in love with this man Charlie."

Carrie Dawn riffled a hand through the shaggy red bangs falling into her eyes and blinked back tears. "But I'm marrying you."

"We'll see," Macon said diplomatically.

Harper had barely caught her breath before another woman, Mirabella Morehead, was seated in the same chair, a scandalously short black leather miniskirt hiking dangerously high on a well-formed thigh. Chunky platform sandals clung to her slender feet, and as she talked, she had a habit of swinging her shoulder-length blond layered hair as if she were a model on a runway. She had such a breathless way of talking that Harper could barely refrain from offering her oxygen. Midway through her conversation with Macon, Mirabella leaned forward, balancing an electronic notepad on her knee, and said, "What I really want is your baby."

To his credit, Macon didn't even look fazed. "My baby?"

"Yes," Mirabella assured him, with another toss of her mane. "Like yesterday. As I said in my letter, I style hair on movie sets. A friend of mine did all the hair for *City Slickers*. Did you see that?" Before Harper or Macon could respond, she continued, "You know how Billy Crystal saves that cow in the creek?"

"Calf," Macon corrected.

"Cow, calf, whatever," returned Mirabella. "The

point is, I just loved how Billy took that little baby home at the end."

"I see," Macon said, a suppressed smile making his mouth twitch madly. "But instead of a calf, you'd like a human?"

"You sounded so sweet!" Mirabella squealed, looking tremendously relieved, her pink-glossed mouth stretching into a smile. "I knew you'd understand."

Harper wasn't sure she did. As Mirabella headed toward the stairs to unpack, Harper sobered. Meeting these women was, by far, the craziest thing in which she'd ever been involved. Surely, nothing could come of this. Macon wasn't about to start a life with one of these women, was he? And yet Harper had seen him watch Cordy, his eyes filling with quiet possession. Was he really going to be a father to their son? And did he want another baby?

Imagining him holding one brought another rush of guilt. Had she known, she'd never have withheld so much. Feeling tied in knots, Harper wished she hadn't set herself up. She'd asked for this, but she felt like a damn fool, watching these women fall all over him. Oblivious, he sighed with satisfaction as they waited for Chantal Morris.

"It's quite a lineup," he said, casually seating himself on the arm of Harper's chair and draping his arm around the back.

"Lineup?" she murmured, knowing his word choice was meant to rile her and wishing she couldn't smell his dark male scent. "Isn't that for criminals, Macon?"

"Or chorus girls."

She shot him a sour glance. "Good thing I'm out of the running. I don't cancan."

His eyes drifted to where the hem of the mint dress brushed her bare knees. "A shame."

Aware he'd trapped her in the big, cushy armchair, she kept her voice even. "We're here to meet the woman you're going to marry." Was doing so giving him the confidence to get too close?

But no. He knew exactly what he was doing, and her heart thudded dully while an ache of loneliness she simply couldn't fight pulled her apart. She couldn't help it. She wanted him, maybe even needed him. "We're trying to find you a wife," she repeated.

His sudden, gentle smile almost hurt. It had been years since he'd looked at her with that much warmth, almost as if he, too, shared her feelings. And his scent was so near and strong, so tempting, that her whole body felt strangely tight.

"I'm not sure that matters," he murmured. "After all, you know how men are, Harper."

She could barely find her voice. "No, how are they?"

"Like bass. Hard to catch."

Before she could form a retort, he angled his head down, lowered his mouth and gave her what she secretly wanted. Harper wasn't proud of it, but recalling how those women had looked at him motivated her to mold her hands over his shoulders, her fingers tingling, warming to chambray and then the skin of his neck. Thick waves of his hair teased her as she pulled him to her, giving in to the impulse to claim him, the firm pressure of his mouth feeling heavenly, the probing need of his tongue evidence of how he wanted her.

A throat was cleared.

Gasping, Harper pulled back her head, reclaimed her hands and nervously pressed fingers to her lips as if to erase the dampness. Macon shot to his feet beside the chair.

Harper's heart tugged. It was Chantal Morris. She was standing stock-still in the doorway. She was seventeen, Harper knew, but since she was petite, she looked even younger. An ill-fitting maternity dress stretched across her full belly, and a tiny gold Christian cross hung around her neck, its chain neatly concealed under the round collar of the dress. With dark, slanting, almond-shaped eyes and lovely, dusky skin as ethereal as smoke, she was an undiscovered beauty, her jaw-length hair straightened but otherwise unstyled. She wore no makeup.

"Mr. McCann," she said in a shocked whisper, "I came all the way from Missouri. I thought you said you wanted to get married. Wasn't that why you wrote to me? Wasn't that why you asked us women to come?"

Macon's eyes filled with compassion rivaling Harper's. "I do want to get married," he assured her gently, and hearing his voice deepening with the solemnity of the words, Harper had to wonder if Macon had only now realized how very real this was. These five women desperately wanted a husband.

Chantal glanced at Harper uncertainly. "But she's not even one of your guests. Who is she?"

"The mother of my son," Macon admitted, shooting Harper a helpless glance. "It's a long story."

Chantal was utterly stunned. "I'll bet it is, Mr. McCann. You didn't say anything about children."

STANDING on the threshold of the room the women were to share, Cordy took in a single cot and four neatly made, roughly hewn bunks, then he stared through white, tie-back curtains to the hills. In the twilight, corralled horses lazed under shade trees, grazing beside a sparkling blue creek, but Cordy knew the comfortable accommodations hardly mattered. Putting these women together was a big mistake.

Not that it could be avoided, he realized, as he watched them unpack. The ranch house was huge, but Cam and Blanche McCann had branched out, using the guest rooms, and with Macon home and Cordy visiting, only one guest room remained. Cordy figured these women would kill each other.

Clearly, they'd come here on a manhunt and weren't in the mood to make friends, and the whole time Cordy had been with them, they'd grilled him about Macon's relationship to his mother. Feeling worn out from carrying all their suitcases upstairs, Cordy scowled at the lime-green trunk covered with Day-Glo stickers, which had nearly broken his back. It was Mirabella's. She was the one from L.A.

They all were so different. The gorgeous Anna, country bumpkin Carrie Dawn, maternal forty-year-old Judith, and Chantal, who was only seventeen and so pregnant that when Cordy first saw her at the airport, he feared he'd wind up taking her to a delivery room, not the ranch.

He never should have offered to help them get settled, but until now, Cordy had thought this whole situation was funny. He just loved watching how frustrated Macon got when Cordy's mom put him in a jam. "Anything else I can get you all?"

Mirabella glared at him. "This is a waste of time. He's not serious about this. I could have gone to the Annual Festival of Unified L.A. Hair Salons this week," she informed him, looking utterly defeated and tossing her Ally McBeal hair indignantly. As discreet airy layers swirled around her cheeks, she threw a black lace teddy into the lime trunk. "Every one of us might as well repack," she continued, casting a disheartened glance around the room and shoving a hand into the back pocket of her miniskirt. "Like, I don't know about you guys, but I regret coming. Maybe I could have met somebody—*a man*—at that festival."

"Face it," returned Judith Stone, the voice of reason. "It's a stereotype, Mirabella, but lots of men in the hair care industry really are gay, which is why you came here instead. Macon *sounded* as if he wanted a wife. He *sounded* as if he might want a baby."

"Well, he doesn't!" Carrie Dawn said venomously, shoving her hands into the pockets of tight jeans before stomping a cowboy boot angrily on the floor. "I'd have better luck wrestling Charlie to the altar!" She heaved a bulging cross-country backpack onto a top bunk, then glanced at Cordy. "Didn't you all see Cordy's mama sitting there?" she asked the other women. "Didn't you get a load of how she was sizing us up?" Carrie Dawn blew out an exasperated sigh. "Dang if I'm leaving, though," she announced, turning to Cordy. "No way. We'll make your daddy marry one of us, Cordy. He has to. It's only fair. He wrote us each a letter saying he would, right?"

"Ab-so-lutely," agreed Mirabella. "We could probably even sue for false advertising. Let's refuse to leave until one of us has a ring on her finger."

"A pop tab will do," Carrie Dawn replied. "I'm not picky. I'm trying to get back at my boyfriend, Charlie. I want to see the look on his face when he realizes I'm married. I want him to see my wedding pictures when I go back to the Mountaineer Equipment Company to finish cleaning out my desk."

Chantal shifted her weight uncomfortably on a lower bunk, a trembling palm gliding slowly over her swollen belly, her reed-thin voice shaking. "You're all so pretty. Especially Anna," she said, glancing at Anna Gonzales. "You won't have any trouble finding husbands. But me..." Her dark, almond-shaped eyes welled with tears. "Well, he'd never want me, anyway. I'm pregnant and African American...and he's white and so much older. Oh, I shouldn't say it," she apologized, her eyes shifting uncertainly to Cordy. "But I...I saw those two kissing."

Carrie Dawn's bright blue eyes widened beneath her red bangs. She gasped. "Macon and Cordy's *mother?* I knew it!"

Cordy stared at Chantal, feeling confused and yet relieved since the women were distracted, and not going for each other's throats. "Kissing?" he asked.

"Your folks," Judith muttered, sounding disappointed as she fluffed her raven curls, her short red nails looking like polka dots in her hair. "No offense, Cordy, but I do wish your father had been a little more straightforward about his situation."

"Like I said," defended Cordy, "Macon didn't know his situation when he wrote to you."

Judith nodded, glancing into her open Louis Vuitton suitcase which, like a Russian nesting toy, was packed, in turn, with ever-smaller identically matching bags. "Well," she added philosophically, "maybe we could view this as a free vacation."

"I need a wedding, not Club Med! I want to make Charlie jealous!" Carrie Dawn began pacing, the movements of her small-breasted, muscular body stealthy as a caged bobcat's. "My marrying Macon's supposed to make Charlie eat his heart out! I already sent him the *Texas Men* ad. Next week, when I clean out my desk at work, I was going to show everybody the wedding pictures, and I figured Charlie would come out of his office and realize everything he's missing."

"Macon—" Anna Gonzales interrupted, speaking with a slight trace of Spanish accent "—he's such a hunk, eh? Straight white teeth. Those big muscles. A wicked sparkle in his eyes." Holding the hem of a white eyelet skirt, she swished it across her knees, her huaraches lightly tapping the floor as she danced a half circle around her embroidered duffel. "What a man, eh?" she said decisively. "Maybe one woman's just not enough for him?" She laughed. "Anyway, Judith is right. Let's have a fun time, huh, girls?"

But how could they? Cordy stared at them, wishing he knew the truth about Macon and his mother. Yesterday, Cordy *thought* he understood the situation. Years ago, Macon had been a friend to Cordy's mom. Earlier this year, Cordy had had sex. He had used a condom, and both he and his girlfriend had known they were only experimenting. Cordy figured it had been the same for his mom. Now he shoved his hands deep into his pockets. "I don't know why they were kissing," he said. "But I don't think it...*means* anything."

"Oh, it means something," Judith assured him.

"Of course it does," agreed Mirabella, as she surveyed Chantal's hair. "Well, we can't color you," she added with a resigned sigh, "not while you're pregnant, but before I leave here, you're getting a weave. I refuse to think I came all the way from Los Angeles for nothing."

Chantal lowered her eyes. "Thanks, really, but I can't afford a weave."

"I'll treat," Judith said.

"No charge," said Mirabella. "I welcome the opportunity to take my mind off our sorry situation."

"Oh, forget our dang hair!" Carrie Dawn burst out, forcing them back to the issue. "We might as well all be as bald as eagles for all the attention Macon paid us. The only woman he's looking at is Cordy's mama."

Mirabella was lifting a bag of hair care products from her trunk. "I just wanted a baby," she said, looking close to tears.

Judith's red-tipped fingers waved through the air in a philosophical gesture, her blue eyes turning sympathetic as they drifted over Chantal. "Well," she murmured, pulling a Western-style shirt from the suitcase and using her teeth to detach dangling price tags. "Apparently, Macon didn't know Cordy was his son when he wrote to us, right?"

Cordy nodded quickly. "I told you everything I

know. I don't think Macon and my mom even talked to each other for years, but..."

"But there must be more going on between those two than they're admitting," Carrie Dawn finished, suddenly seating herself next to Chantal on the bunk bed. "I swear," she continued, confiding in Chantal, "this is way wilder than what was happening with me and Charlie. I don't feel half as guilty about being stupid enough to fall for my boss."

"And how do you feel about this, Cordy?" Judith asked calmly. "Do you want your parents to get together?"

Cordy stared at her, his jaw dropping. "No!"

Mirabella's voice caught with hope. "Are you sure?"

In truth, he'd have to think about it. He'd gotten to know Macon. Cordy respected how he ran his construction business in Houston and how he worked the ranch, but Macon had an awfully bad reputation as a womanizer. Not that Cordy could share that with a bunch of women who'd come here to marry him. Surely, Macon would settle down once he was married, Cordy told himself.

But Macon and his mother? Together? No way. Years ago, when his mom was really young and foolish, she'd had one wild night and had fallen for Macon's considerable charms. But she was Cordy's mom, which meant that, later, she'd wised up.

Cordy sighed, avoiding the question. "You're all real nice," he began, "so I'm sorry about this."

"It's not your fault, sweetheart," said Judith.

"Gosh," gushed Mirabella guiltily. "Don't think

we're mad at you, Cordy. You're real sweet. Thanks for picking us all up at the airport."

"And bringing our bags upstairs," Anna said.

"Dang," added Carrie Dawn. "Who knew we'd come here looking for a husband and get embroiled in such a big scandal? First a man advertises for a wife, then he finds out he was a daddy for sixteen years and didn't even know it." She shook her head. "I'm telling you," she declared, "Charlie would have appreciated this. He has a sense of irony."

Mirabella sat on Judith's bunk. "I know it's selfish," she complained, "but why couldn't things work out right for once? Why couldn't he be available?"

"He *is*," Cordy assured her, thinking these women couldn't be more wrongheaded.

But his potential stepmothers didn't look convinced. And glancing around, Cordy realized he could probably grow to like them all, despite how they'd initially annoyed him. Mirabella desperately wanted a baby to love, and Judith missed her kids, who were off at college. It sounded as if Charlie deserved his comeuppance from Carrie Dawn, but somebody had to take care of Chantal and her coming child. Anna was so drop-dead gorgeous that it would be a sin if some man didn't have her. Besides, she'd confessed in the car that she needed a green card.

"Don't worry," Cordy suddenly said, his heart pulling in a way it hadn't since his dad died. "I've got an in with Macon." Pausing, Cordy registered the truth in what he had said, feeling faintly embarrassed over how hard Macon was trying to make up for lost years. He needed to slow down, give Cordy some space and let things take their course. On the other hand, right about now, Macon would do anything Cordy asked—maybe even marry.

"You've got an in?" Carrie Dawn sounded hopeful.

Cordy nodded. "I'll make sure he marries one of you." But who? Each woman needed a husband so badly....

"Really," whispered Mirabella. "You'll help us, Cordy?"

Cordy warmed to the idea. "Sure."

"One of us will marry, and the others will promise to be bridesmaids," said Mirabella. "That seems fair. And I'll do everybody's hair."

"I'll take Chantal shopping." Before the girl could protest, Judith added, "I'm rich as sin, sweetheart, and I love to shop. We're going to make this a wonderful week for you."

"I can do your makeup, too," Mirabella said, her features brightening. "You know that movie *The Bodyguard?* Well, I went to beauty school with the woman who did Whitney Houston."

Chantal's eyes widened. "No kidding?"

With a long, airbrushed fingernail, Mirabella drew an X on her chest. "Cross my heart."

"That's the spirit," Carrie Dawn said, suddenly laughing. "I need to forget Charlie for a while. This just might turn out to be fun."

"I'll start doing a little matchmaking," Cordy assured them, slowly glancing around the room, wondering which woman he should convince his father to marry.

6

"SAVING THIS DANCE for somebody special?"

"No, and if you don't take it, I'll wind up being the only unmarried woman here who wasn't your partner tonight." Harper's gaze panned the dimly lit, festively decorated interior of the McCann barn before settling on Macon, and she fought a smile as he leaned, captured her hand and threaded strong, tanned fingers through hers. *He would*, she thought, an unaccountable rush of pleasure mixing with pique. He was the only man she knew who consistently took her sparring tone as a personal invitation to get physical.

"Of course I've had a lot of partners," Macon responded, looking vaguely relieved to escape them as he and Harper passed the buffet tables and hit the packed dirt that was serving as a dance floor. "That's the point of the dance, isn't it? I'm supposed to be choosing my bride."

Even though Harper was aiding and abetting, the idea kept rankling. "Don't let me keep you from socializing."

"You're not. Besides, I *have* been socializing."

At his annoyed tone, she bit back a smile. While she didn't necessarily want to take advantage of his discomfort, this was largely a situation of his own making. *And yours*, admitted a little voice inside her. "I do believe I overheard you and Mirabella having a heated discussion about your hairstyle." She couldn't resist drawling. "Now, Macon, do you really think you could talk about such subjects for a lifetime?"

"About hair?" Wincing, Macon paused in front of a table where his friend Ansel Walters was playing disc jockey. "No," he admitted. "Mirabella says she wants me to grow mine long and let her paint in some silver streaks."

Harper laughed. "Sounds very L.A. Judith told me she wants to take you shopping."

Macon shot Harper a long, level glance with wickedly narrowed amber eyes before he rolled them heavenward. "Near as I can tell, Judith shops so much, she doesn't have time for marriage."

"Somebody has to pick out the tuxedos."

"She does say she loves to see men wearing suits. I told her I don't even know a cowboy who owns one."

Harper's lips twitched. "And then Judith said...?"

"That I could be the first."

"Now, now," crooned Harper. "Surely there's at least one suit in the back of your closet, Macon."

His eyes glinted with pure devilment. "There is, but I'd just hate to get it dirty and wrinkled before my wedding, Harper."

The wedding. Supposedly, it was only days away, and Harper was feeling increasingly convinced that Macon might be stubborn enough to go through with it. But surely, he wouldn't.

"That," he suddenly muttered, "or my father's funeral."

Fear shot through her. "Has something happened to Cam?"

Macon shrugged as they headed into the thick of the crowd, weaving beneath crepe paper streamers and through a sea of denim and cowboy boots. "He's fine, but he had a scare earlier today, so he couldn't come tonight. His blood pressure shot up, all the way into the stroke range, and Diego wound up running him to the emergency room."

Harper stopped in her tracks. How could they be dancing when Cam was in trouble? "Diego took him to the hospital?"

"Yeah. Cam said he couldn't stand having his own family fussing over him. Knowing Diego, he probably rerouted them into Big Grisly's Grill on the way for a shot and a beer. When it comes to some things, Diego hasn't got the common sense God gave a plow horse."

Harper's lips parted. "I hadn't heard about this! Cordy didn't say anything."

"Cam doesn't want anybody to know. There's nothing he hates more than pity. He says the attention makes him feel weak and enfeebled." Macon cursed softly. "As much as I hate to admit it, Harper, he *is* weak and enfeebled."

She couldn't believe it. "Is he still at the hospital?"

"No. You know Cam. He wouldn't stay there if they paid him. No doubt, he went out screaming that he wouldn't eat rubber chicken and canned pudding for dinner. He's back home in bed. Our housekeeper stayed to take care of him." Macon thrust a hand raggedly through his already mussed, wavy hair and released a long, frustrated sigh. "Anyway, Doc Dickens rushed to the hospital and got Cam's pressure back down. He's fine." Macon let loose another soft curse. "At least he will be if I can get him to let me start running the ranch." Macon glanced at Harper, his eyes warming. "Thanks for caring to ask."

Of course she cared. Didn't he know that? Guilt coursed through her when she thought about Cordy, and her heart missed a beat as Macon squeezed between the other couples, then pulled her close. The barn was dark and cavernous and, glancing around, Harper felt like the proverbial girl walking through a forest at night with curious eyes watching her from the shadows. News of Cordy's paternity was still circulating, so every eye in the place was unabashedly glued to her and Macon.

"We'd better cool it, Macon," she suddenly warned, too aware that he was drawing her snugly against him, curling her hand on his chest instead of holding it aloft.

She supposed sheer perversity made Macon yank her ever nearer. "You think I care what people think?"

"No." She tried to ignore how soft his blue chambray shirt felt beneath her fingertips, then how hungrily a work-callused hand glided down her back. "But you should, Macon."

He grinned at her. "Well, I don't."

"Obviously not," she managed to say on a sigh. He was holding her in the tight, possessive way he always did—the way her tortured imagination had long ago convinced her he'd held so many other women. Spicy heat seeped from his palm, through her dress, then straight into her blood, and it didn't help that, only days ago, she'd worn this same white dress embroidered with bluebonnets. Didn't help that from the assessing, unapologetic way his eyes studied the low-cut neckline, he was obviously remembering how easily he'd flicked open each small white button. "Love that dress," he murmured as if reading her mind.

Damn her own soul, but Harper had meant for him to. "This old dress?" she asked casually. "Why, I couldn't find a thing to wear. Pulled it from the back of the closet at the very last minute."

A low throaty rumble of satisfied laughter that could only be called rakish sounded over Willie Nelson's "Always on my Mind." "Keep it up and you just might put a stop to my wedding, Harper."

Despite her innocent smile, her breath caught. "Now, how could I do that?"

His gaze seared her. "By making a dishonest man of me."

She tried not to look too pleased. "I'm tempting you?"

"Like the worst kind of seductress," he returned, lazily guiding her around other dancers. The scent of citrus clung to the clean-shaven jaw that grazed her cheek, but a hint of stubble was there, too, just a grating rasp against fairer skin. He hummed along with the music, sounding chesty and out of tune, his low-voiced, hoarse whisper coming in tandem with Willie's melodious notes. "Tell me that your sweet love never died...."

Was Macon only singing with the music? Or was he asking her if she still had feelings for him? Tilting her head back a fraction, she stared into Macon's eyes, looking for answers. She should have known she'd only find smoke and raw, unguarded heat. Only inches away, his eyes burned—all golden fire and intensity—and just as she registered that, she felt the hard muscles of his shoulders quiver. Suddenly, his shirt felt too warm beneath her hands, too damp from so much dancing. Dangerous male musk shot to the core of her, and for an instant, her sandaled feet felt drunken. She swayed, her fingers tightening reflexively, digging hard into his shoulders.

"Don't hurt me," he warned huskily, not meaning it, not bothering to hide his amusement at her momentary lapse of control. Playfully, he jerked his head toward the punch table, his seductive drawl turning to a taunt. "Aren't you afraid you'll make my guests mad?"

Her heart was racing. "Mad?"

He nodded. "Yeah. By holding me so tightly?"

Only moments before, she'd told Macon they should cool it. Now she managed an unconcerned glance, not relinquishing her hold. "I'm a big girl," she retorted lightly. "I guess I'll take my chances with your myriad girlfriends."

His mouth quirked, his lips curling at the corners, his eyes still hot with something more dangerous than mild amusement. "Well," he warned, "if they start trying to scratch your eyes out, don't count on me to defend you, Harper."

"If I'm lucky, maybe they'll stop at killer glances."

His chuckle was rich, inviting. "They're definitely shooting you those."

Anna wasn't. She was busy dancing with Diego, and Mirabella was learning the two-step from a cowboy who worked at Ansel's ranch. But Carrie Dawn, Judith and Cordy were huddled near a washtub packed with ice and cold long-necked beers, glaring at Macon and Harper. Chantal's expression was harder to read. She was nearly lost in the dim light, either her dusky skin or tenuous uncertainty making her fade into the darkness of the crowds and barn wall. Closer, Harper could see others from town, among them Lois Potts. All were staring at her and Macon with blatant curiosity.

Harper sighed. "They're watching our every move, Macon."

"Good moves, too."

Definitely. Macon's body fit to hers like a glove. Not that it mattered, Harper thought with a vague undercurrent of panic. Macon really had spent the evening entertaining his female guests. Did he truly intend to marry one of them? And even if he didn't want to, did he have a choice, given that Cam wouldn't turn over the ranch unless Macon went through with it?

"No doubt, Cordy'll cut in soon," Macon was saying. "I figure he thinks I should be dancing with Judith. Yesterday, when we went on that hayride, he made sure I sat next to her. I think he likes her best. She's older. Probably she'd make the best stepmother."

Was Macon soliciting her opinion or merely goading her, inciting her to confess her feelings? Unsure, she said nothing, just drew in a quick, surreptitious breath as he unlaced their fingers, then dropped his hand, leaving both free to clutch her hips. Fingertips pressed into her, guiding her a crucial inch closer, forcing their hips to lock.

He was aroused. Very, very aroused. Awareness of it sent her senses reeling, as did the sharp scent of him brought by another intake of breath. Smells of burned marshmallows and hot dogs wafted through the open barn doors, too, and as Macon danced with her toward the night air, she was glad, since she seemed to have lost every ounce of her breath and could use some air. She could see the bonfire outside, shooting snapping red sparks into a cooling velvet sky. Cowboys were gathered in groups, their boots resting on the tailgates of their trucks, no doubt talking about beef prices.

Earlier, she'd watched Macon dance with every woman present until her wish to hold him became a slow-burning ache. Now, feeling him so insufferably close, his hard, muscular body swaying in time with hers, she longed to know what was happening between them. Was he beginning to forgive her for not telling him about Cordy? Did he know she'd change the past if she could? And was he really getting married this week?

One thing was certain. He'd never stop wanting her. His eyelids had lowered, and his eyes were tracing breasts she was certain he was desperate to touch. She felt every nuance of the gaze, as she would a finger across her skin. What would be the harm of running off with him tonight? she suddenly wondered, her mind feeling fuzzy.

And then she glanced at Cordy. No doubt, things were already confusing enough for him. Not to mention for Macon's prospective brides, who'd come here hoping to marry him.

Which they will, she thought. *If he doesn't get married, Cam's health will fail.* Cam's trip to the hospital tonight made that even more of a reality.

Macon was watching her. "You did a great job putting this party together, Harper."

She blushed at the unexpected compliment. "I had a lot of help." Her eyes sparkled, a hint of teasing wickedness breaking the mood. "There seems to be a vested interest in getting you married off, Macon. Even Nancy Ludell helped decorate the barn."

Macon nodded, looking amused. When he spoke, his tone was dry. "And don't forget our new schoolteacher, Betsy. I heard she made the rum punch."

Neither of them mentioned Lois Potts. "Maybe they're hoping you'll change your mind and marry a local girl, after all."

Are you *hoping?* Macon's eyes seemed to ask. Right now, she felt as if she was falling in love with him all over again, not that she trusted this wary truce.

"Unfortunately," he continued in a hushed tone, the slow trail of his eyes indicating he wasn't entirely oblivious to her thoughts, "I think my friend Sheriff Brown is checking out Anna Gonzales's papers."

Harper lowered her voice. "Cordy told me she's in the country illegally."

Macon dipped his head a fraction, and the husky hum of his breath stirred against her ear. "She wants a green card, and she might succeed yet. Diego's got a hell of a crush on her."

Harper frowned. "He's too old for Anna!"

Macon shrugged. "What's age got to do with love?"

She could barely believe she was here, dancing with Macon, talking about love. "Nothing, I guess. I did hear them talking earlier."

"Saying?"

Harper shrugged. "Who knows? It was in Spanish."
She smiled. "Chantal looks great."

Macon nodded, the fingers he'd threaded through
Harper's tightening as he turned. "I'm glad Mirabella
did her hair, if for no other reason than it kept her
hands off mine."

Chantal's was pulled away from her face, length-
ened by hair extensions and falling in braids, which lay
tightly to her head until reaching her nape, where they
were gathered into coiled, beaded strands. For the first
time, her long, swanlike neck was visible, and blusher
brought out proud, high cheekbones. "She wouldn't
let Judith take her shopping, but they compromised,
going through that second-hand store on South Dallas."

Macon squinted into the darkness. "That's a second-
hand dress?"

Harper's smile widened. "Pretty, isn't it?" It was
light pink and gathered beneath the teenager's breasts,
leaving the nearly ankle-length crepe skirt to flow over
her full belly. "Her parents sound like really good people," Harper continued, frowning, since as much as
she'd intended to befriend Chantal, it hadn't been easy.
It was irrational, yes, but the fact remained that Chantal, like the other women, had come here to marry Macon. Cordy had befriended her, though, and from him,
Harper had learned more about her situation.

"Good people?" Anger laced Macon's words. "If
Chantal's folks are such good people, they'd never
have tossed her out of her house in Missouri like that."

Glancing up, Harper surveyed him a moment. Evidence of some hard living was etched into the deep

grooves by his mouth, and the dark flecks marring his eyes suddenly made them look like old gold coins that had passed through many hands. "They didn't toss her out, Macon," she said.

"Maybe not," Macon admitted. "But they're not supporting her. To be seventeen, pregnant and trying to finish school has got to be tough."

Harper stiffened. "It was."

He cursed under his breath. "I didn't mean you, Harper."

"But it was for me." She hadn't even wanted to tell her girlfriends, for fear they'd shun her as Chantal's friends had. "Her parents just don't know how to handle it. My mother sure didn't."

Looking stunned, Macon edged closer to the barn door, where the cooler night air blew inside. "She knew?"

"I told her."

He knew how her mother was: intrusive, controlling, full of dire predictions about everything from Harper's future prospects to the rising price of eggs. She'd been Chicken Little, the sky always falling.

"I shouldn't have told her," Harper admitted. "You know how she was. Everything was the end of the world."

"Why did you?"

"I was getting sick in the morning, so she knew, anyway. It was better to have it out in the open."

Macon's arms tightened around her, and heat as soothing as menthol flooded everywhere their bodies touched. Suddenly, none of this even seemed possible. Were they really in the McCanns' barn, dancing? Talking about the secrets of their past, the conception of the son they were trying to share? And all while five visiting women hoped to become his bride? "How can a week move so fast?" she whispered.

"Seven days, each twenty-four hours. But it feels like a bolt of lightning," he agreed.

The dance had ended, too. Somehow, the song "Always on my Mind" had turned into "Angel Flying too Close to the Ground." Harper realized they'd stopped near the barn door and were barely moving anymore. Her voice seemed lost, lodged in her throat. "Your mother already ordered flowers for the altar, Macon," she found herself saying. "And she's found an organist."

For the first time, he looked genuinely disturbed. "Is getting married like this even legal, Harper?"

"What do you mean?"

He shrugged. "To get blood tests so soon before you're married? Isn't there a waiting period or something?"

"I don't know," she said truthfully.

He looked surprised. "You were married."

"And very stressed," she countered. When unexpected compassion filled his eyes, she continued. "Pine Hills is a small town, you know. And your daddy does happen to own quite a lot of it."

Macon smirked. "Harper, it's not as if Cam's got the minister in his pocket."

"No. But Cam and Reverend Shute *do* fish together."

The comment only increased Macon's discomfort. "Along with Doc Dickens and the justice of the peace," he said.

She fought it, but her heart was feeling too big for her chest. "Getting nervous, Macon?" God, she hoped he was.

"That, or I need a break from all the activity." He stepped back, his hand found hers again, and he pulled her through the open barn doors into the night.

As the cooler air hit her cheeks, her breath caught. "Where are you taking me, Macon?"

"I HAVEN'T been up here in years," Macon said a half hour later, swerving the truck around, then backing toward the bluff so the truck bed faced a steep drop-off.

"Star Point," Harper murmured.

Resting a hand on the headrest behind her, Macon turned, glancing through the back windshield and staring down the ribbon of road they'd just traversed. His eyes followed where it snaked down Pine Cone Mountain, the narrow, red-dirt strip widening, turning to gray gravel, then to two lanes of newly laid pavement as black as freshly turned coal. It was lush up here, and cooler, with the heavy boughs of oaks, mesquites and sycamores thick with summer leaves that arched over the truck, creating a canopy. The mosquitoes didn't seem too bad. Through his open window, Macon heard the sudden splash of a fish in the nearby lake. "C'mon."

Harper squinted. "Where?"

"To the back of the truck, to look at the stars." Before she could protest, Macon reached behind the seat and grabbed a plaid duvet and two pillows. He got out, plucking a blade of grass from the ground as he circled the truck. He thrust it between his lips as he let down the tailgate. Just as he hopped in back, the dome light snapped on again when she opened her door. Glancing up as he laid out the duvet, he got a faint impression of her—of shadows on her cheeks and neck—then she slammed the door and was swallowed by darkness. Twigs snapped under her feet, then she appeared below him. Chewing thoughtfully on the weed, he thrust a hand down. "Here."

Even though they'd come here together countless times when they were teens, she hesitated, then grabbed his hand. Electricity shot through him as her fingers closed around his, then he felt another jolt as she wedged a foot to the tailgate for leverage. As he hauled her up, her dress slipped high on her thigh, and simply seeing a flash of panty felt like more than Macon could bear. Then Harper was standing there, backlit by a three-quarter moon and incredible array of stars. He lay down on the blanket, shoved a pillow behind his head, clasped his hands behind his neck and surveyed her, thoughtfully chewing the blade of grass.

Her voice sounded strangely unsteady. "I'm not sure I trust a man who keeps bedding in his truck."

Macon chuckled. "It's probably wise not to," he admitted, talking around the grass blade. Her sudden smile took his breath. He added, "And the way you look right now, Harper, you definitely shouldn't trust me."

"No?"

Shaking his head, he drawled, "No. And by the way, you're blocking the moon."

"Pity," she murmured with mock contrition, seating herself next to him. A second later, she was lying beside him on her back, her hands folded beneath her breasts in a way that accentuated their fullness and made him imagine how they'd look covered by his dark hands.

"Funny," she said, staring at the stars, oblivious to his thoughts. "I haven't been up here for years. So many things have changed, but Star Point's exactly the same."

Macon nodded. So many years had passed. Harper had spent sixteen of them with another man, and a son Macon didn't know about had nearly grown up during that time. Damn right, things had changed. But here, the sky was still liquid velvet. The stars shone bright and white against a backdrop of the blackest ink. Only a few tiny lights twinkled far down the mountain, reminding him that Pine Hills, despite all the drama he and Harper shared, remained nothing more than a nowhere town in the middle of the Texas wilderness.

She seemed to read his mind. "I know you came back because of Cam, Macon. Is it okay? Do you miss Houston?"

He started to say he'd only gone there because she'd married Bruce, but he didn't. Instead, he thought of the impressive skyline, the jagged peaks of buildings blocking out the stars, and then said a truth that surprised him. "Not even a little, Harper. I thought I would, but I don't."

She nodded, suddenly shivering. "Now I remember that it was always ten degrees colder up here."

"Here. We're in the mountains. Put this on." Unbuttoning his shirt, Macon sat just long enough to shrug out of it, then he lay down again, his tongue lazily toying with the blade of grass as he watched Harper draw the shirt around her shoulders.

She glanced at him. "It's soft," she murmured, a lock of her upswept hair falling as she rubbed her cheek against the chambray. "Sure you'll be warm enough?"

"The night air feels good." The only thing that would feel better would be her fingers. Somehow, he was glad she was taking in the scent of his sweat-damp shirt, sharing the warmth of fabric heated by his body. His eyes were adjusting enough to see the confused emotion in her eyes. It was something he shared. By rights, he should be sore as hell at her. Not telling him about a son was something a man could never forgive.

Instead he found himself wordlessly wrapping an arm around her shoulders and pulling her to him. Just as wordlessly, Harper came, curling against him, her cheek brushing his chest, the soft breeze blowing her silken hair across him. Briefly cupping her shoulder, he drifted a hand down until it splayed on her back. What were they doing up here? he suddenly wondered. Together. Alone. In the dark. Why had he left a party where five women were waiting, hoping to get to know him?

"Star Point," Harper whispered, something that sounded suspiciously like pain in her voice. "Why'd you bring me up here, Macon?"

His chest felt tight. "Because we used to come here."

Slowly, she traced a heart near his solar plexus. Her voice was low, throaty. "We did more than just come up here."

Lying with her in the moonlight, he suddenly realized this was most likely where Cordy was conceived.

Willing himself to move on, he pushed aside the trace of anger, then turned in the hard metal truck bed and gazed at her. He lifted a hand, tugged the grass blade from his mouth, tossed it aside and said, "I want to know what happened."

"What happened?"

Glancing away, he found himself staring into the black night again, into stars as magical as Harper's eyes. He should have known he'd never really leave this town. Forget Houston. Home was here. His heart was here. It was on Star Point, where the moon always looked so close you could touch it. It was here, with Harper. His eyes found hers again, and his fingers brushed a cheek as smooth as glass, as soft as silk. "Were you going to run away with me, the way you said you would?"

She surveyed him honestly. "I don't know, Macon."

It was hardly what he wanted to hear. "Why not?"

"That night, I was going to tell you about the baby...about Cordy. I'd just found out. Later, I wasn't so sure. I got another home pregnancy test, in case the results weren't the same."

"But they were?"

She nodded slowly. "Yeah."

His throat felt tight. "Were you happy about the baby?"

She glanced at the stars. "Later, I was happy," she said, the usual tartness gone from her voice. "After I got married. I guess I felt secure enough to be happy then. Before, I was just scared, Macon. You know how it was. I was seventeen when he was born. Mama wasn't exactly the most understanding woman in the world." Her eyes found his, and she sighed. "It's why I feel so much for Chantal."

His voice didn't break, but he half expected it to. "Couldn't you have talked to me?"

She looked startled. "I was going to tell you that night, but like I said before, Mama caught me leaving the house. I finally went to meet you, anyway. I just pushed past her. Then I wound up walking all the way down to Big Grisly's Grill."

Macon shouldn't have been there, but some of the wilder kids would hang around outside in the parking lot. "Nothing happened between Lois and me that night, Harper."

"That's not how it looked to me."

Her eyes said she knew the truth, that he and Lois had done everything but. "I thought you'd stood me up," he said, knowing it was no excuse. Recalling his youthful foolishness, he felt a rush of anger, now directed at her mama for being so strict and filling Harper with so much fear and so many lies that she'd never trust men. Then he silently cursed himself for not having been more trustworthy. "Maybe you were right to have faith in Bruce, not me."

"I don't know if I really did at first, Macon," she whispered, her lips parting in astonishment. "But...I was in his new pharmacy in Opossum Creek, buying a pregnancy test, and I wound up breaking down and telling him everything."

And he'd offered her a way out.

I was going to marry you, Harper. Pride kept Macon from saying it. His eyes drifted over her face. All she'd been through—motherhood and widowhood, not to mention plain old everyday living—hadn't really changed her much, the way he'd imagined it would. For him, she was like Star Point. Never changing. A constant in his life. His hand was still splayed on her back, and he harshly drew a breath as he glided his fingers slowly upward, over the body he'd loved so many times. He touched her belly, the plump curve of a breast, feeling pure male possession when the nipple tightened. Finally, he found her shoulder and, cupping it, drew her closer.

Insects whirred in the trees. There was another splash from the lake, the rustle of leaves, the strained sound of his and Harper's mingling breath. He brought his mouth to hers then, ever so slowly, emotion filling him. He wasn't sure what the kiss meant or where their relationship was heading. Days ago, he'd been desperate to marry a stranger, just to get Harper out of his system. He'd been sure one of the five visiting women would appeal to him. Now, he was just as sure he could only marry Harper.

Dammit, it had always been Harper.

7

"YOU SAID you'd help us, Cordy!" Carrie Dawn's denim skirt ballooned as she plopped down miserably on a lower bunk in the room the women were sharing. "We agreed to work together, and you said you were going to do some matchmaking. You promised! But the week's nearly over, and we're getting nowhere!"

"Calm down!" Cordy exclaimed, managing to close the door. "Or Macon'll hear you. I think that was his truck in the driveway. He's probably downstairs. I think he just came in."

"Smelling of your mama's perfume!" Carrie Dawn sniped, rapidly fanning her face as if unaware the air conditioner was going full blast. Stopping, she fidgeted distractedly, briefly toying with the straps of a tank top that was the same red as her hair. "I wore a *skirt* to that stupid barn dance!" she said, exploding again. "And I never wear skirts! Your daddy didn't even notice! He only danced with me once!" Tears welled in her blue eyes. "How can I make Charlie jealous if nobody else even wants me?"

Cordy barely heard the tirade. He liked Carrie Dawn just fine, and he was sorry the women were upset again, but he was much more concerned that his own mother had driven off with Macon earlier. Sure, she'd known Macon in the past—Cordy had already leapfrogged around that emotional mine field—but she'd been young then. Stupid. Unaware of what kind of man would make the best husband. Then she'd wised up and married Bruce, Cordy's dad. Now, unfortunately, she was a widow, and that meant trouble. Cordy might be only sixteen, but even he knew widows were extra lonely and therefore easy prey for charming men like Macon.

Cordy's mother and Macon had last been seen by Ansel's cowhand Jeff Davis, who was late coming to the barn dance and had passed them on South Dallas Street, just outside Happy Licks Ice Cream Parlor. Even worse, someone said Macon's truck had been headed up Pine Cone Mountain toward Star Point. Cordy knew Star Point like the back of his hand, as did every healthy sixteen-year-old male in Pine Hills, which was exactly why Cordy couldn't imagine his mother had ever gone there, at least not before tonight. Probably, when Macon lured her up there, Cordy's poor, clueless, defenseless mom had really thought Macon wanted to show her the stars or some such nonsense.

Cordy could almost hear Macon talking about the view, dangling the scenery in front of her like a carrot. *Why, you've never seen the stars till you've seen them from a place called Star Point, Harper.* Cordy ground his teeth, hot to know exactly what Macon had done to his mother during the three-hour absence. Should Cordy charge downstairs and demand that Macon tell him?

Cordy scowled, taking in the discarded clothes strewn across the bunk beds as he removed his straw hat and placed it on a dresser, using the brim to edge aside Mirabella's Velcro bouffant rollers. "Look, Carrie Dawn," Cordy finally began, "I know I said I'd try to fix one of you up with Macon, but—"

"A-yeah, but we need to move on, Cordy," Anna Gonzales interjected, her black eyes flashing with determination. "That man who works for Macon, that man Diego, well, he seems interested in maybe being a husband, so I can't be messing around here anymore. Not with Macon McCann, who isn't really looking for a wife, the way his letter said he was. My sisters, they live in the U.S. already, and I want to be with them." Under her breath, Anna added, "Diego might help me get a green card, too, at least if that Sheriff Brown doesn't run off and call INS."

"I was so excited about getting a fresh start," Judith murmured, disheartened, a faraway look in her blue eyes as she absently finger combed her dark curly hair with freshly manicured, hot-pink nails. "Ever since my marriage broke up and my kids left home, I've felt...felt so lost. Work just isn't fulfilling enough anymore." She forced a smile, glancing around the room. "I confess that I, too, was hoping Macon would become genuinely interested in me. He and I are the closest in age. And, well, once you've been married and had kids, you get used to fussing over people, you know."

"Macon's more the independent type, anyhow," Cordy reminded her. "Besides, maybe things'll still work out."

"It's sweet of you to say so." Judith drew a deep, fortifying breath. "But we all know Macon's not interested in me. Anyway, you've hit the nail on the head. I don't really need another husband."

Cordy's eyebrows shot upward. "You don't?"

"No." Judith shook her head decisively. "Just some poor souls who won't mind if I worry over them a bit."

"Taking them soup when they're sick," moaned Carrie Dawn.

"And ice cream," agreed Chantal wistfully.

"Oh, that's why I've got to have a baby soon! I want to take care of somebody." Mirabella tugged a halter top from her lime-green trunk, then stood in front of a mirror, modeling it with bell-bottom jeans, turning this way and that. "Believe it or not," she continued, "I get tired of having nothing to fuss about in L.A. except myself. That's why I think Anna's right about not waiting to see if Macon's serious or not. Personally, I don't think he'll really announce a bride at the end of the week, which is why I'm glad I met a cute guy tonight."

Carrie Dawn's jaw dropped. "I didn't even think of using a man other than Macon to make Charlie jealous," she said with a groan. "There's a whole forest, and I'm looking at one tree."

"Ah, Mirabella!" Anna laughed. "Are you talking about that cowboy you were dancing with all night? He was no cute guy. He was a stud."

"Girlfriend," added Chantal, glancing at Mirabella and loosening up for the first time, as if the new hairstyle and wardrobe had brought her fresh confidence, "you two were dancing so close I never even got a look at that man."

"His name's Jeff Davis," Mirabella announced excitedly, tossing the halter into her trunk and sitting next to Carrie Dawn, "and he works at the next ranch over, for a man named Ansel Walters. Jeff says he's pretty sure Ansel's about to make him a cow boss, too." She shot Cordy an apologetic glance. "Maybe someone like Jeff's a better bet for me, Cordy. I really want a baby, and your dad...well, he's pushing forty, right?"

Feeling relieved to have Mirabella out of the way, since it would make his life less complex, Cordy managed to say, "Right."

"Forty!" Carrie Dawn exclaimed. "Judith's forty, and Charlie's even older. That doesn't mean anything. Why, Charlie and I could still have had babies." Forgetting herself, she glared at Cordy. "If Charlie had wanted them. Not that we'll ever know now."

"Look here," Cordy defended. "I tried to match-make."

"Well," Carrie Dawn returned, looking once more on the verge of tears, "it didn't work, did it, Cordy?"

Cordy's temper was already on a short fuse. "Maybe not. But if you'd been a little better at coming on to Macon, Carrie Dawn, then things would be working out a whole lot better for me."

Everyone fell silent.

Carrie Dawn miserably confessed, "I guess 'cause I'm in love with Charlie, my heart's just not into seducing Macon."

"Better for you?" Judith was squinting at Cordy. "What do you mean by that?"

How could they be so dense? "If Macon was falling for one of you," Cordy explained, "then he wouldn't have run off with my mother tonight!"

Carrie Dawn leaped to her feet, her fingers covering

her mouth. "Oh, Cordy. I didn't think about it that way. I keep almost forgetting that she's your mother."

"She is. And they were gone for three hours," said Cordy moodily. Presumably, the damage was already done. Three hours was a long time to stay up on Star Point. Cordy's male ardor hadn't lasted anywhere near three hours with Arlene Kendall, whose virginity he'd taken up there. And Cordy was years younger than Macon. Cordy sighed. "It's okay, Carrie Dawn. Forget about it."

Judith was watching him thoughtfully. "Does it really bother you that they spent time together, Cordy? They are your mother and father, after all."

He glanced through the window at the three-quarter moon and stars scattered across the sky. In the distance, he could see random sparks rising from the still-burning bonfire at the barn; the ranch hands would enjoy the fire awhile longer, then douse it with water. He shrugged. "I guess it doesn't," he admitted, frowning. "Not really. But I'd have to get used to the idea. I never thought about my mom and Macon getting together." Pausing, he chewed thoughtfully on his inner cheek. "I probably shouldn't tell you all this," he added, "but I'm worried. Macon's...kind of wild."

"Very," agreed Judith, not looking the least disturbed.

"An animal," pronounced Anna with a generous laugh.

"A major flirt," added Mirabella.

"Too dang charming for his own good, if you ask me," said Carrie Dawn angrily.

"Whatever they shared tonight obviously started

years ago," Judith said on a sigh, her eyes warming as she looked at Cordy. "Earlier, watching them dancing together, I thought they seemed made for each other."

Cordy knew exactly what Judith meant, unfortunately. On the dance floor, his mother had melded to Macon like a melting candlestick. She'd stared at him, her eyes sparkling, her skin glowing, and Cordy had to admit she'd looked happy for the first time in years. He tried not to remember how, after his father died, he'd hear her crying late into the night when she thought he was asleep.

"I know we all came here hoping to get married," said Chantal, slowly rubbing a hand over her curving belly. "But that's probably not going to work out for us."

"No, I think Macon's in love with Cordy's mama," agreed Carrie Dawn, raking her fingers through cropped hair that, in the lamplight, looked more orange than red.

"That's taking things a little far," countered Cordy, frowning worriedly. "But do you think so?"

Chantal nodded. "That's why we should *all* play matchmaker."

Cordy scratched his head, not sure he liked where this was heading. "Huh?"

"We should get your folks together," announced Chantal.

Macon and his mom were doing a fine job without their help, Cordy thought dryly, but he said, "Let me think about it. They'll both be at the pool party tomorrow." Flinging Macon and his mom together was a strange proposition, but maybe if she had her own distractions, she wouldn't smother Cordy so much. Besides, Macon *was* the first man in two years to bring the light back into his mother's eyes.

IT'S EASY, HARPER. Just grab the towels you came in here for and head out the door. Instead, she said, "You again," her tone dry as she glanced around the McCann bathhouse.

"No escaping me," quipped Macon.

"There hasn't been today. You must be stalking me."

"Panting after you," he agreed, "but it's not of my doing, Harper."

No, every time she turned around, her son and Macon's female guests were inexplicably urging Harper into Macon's arms. Not that Harper minded when her eyes drifted over Macon. Dark plaid trunks rode low on his hips, loose enough not to look suggestive, tight enough to make her drool. The trunks were damp and clinging, just as her black two-piece suit was, and she could see the bold masculine curve of him; every other inch was bare, exposing broad shoulders, work-honed biceps chiseled in bronze and gloriously thick chest hairs she'd nestled in last night.

Feeling a sudden need to steady herself, she reached out, resting her fingertips on the windowsill. Last night, nothing much had happened. Harper supposed she had that to be thankful for. Oh, they'd kissed. But otherwise, they'd lain in the truck, staring at the stars and talking, just as they had in the old days when Macon would dream out loud about going away to school and then starting his own business. No, nothing had happened. Trouble was, Harper had *wanted* things to happen.

Lots of things.

He was watching her carefully. "Sure this isn't a setup?"

She squinted at him against the bright white sunlight streaming through the window. "Setup?"

"Seems you're trying to steal a private moment with me."

She arched an eyebrow. "Do you mind terribly?"

Macon suddenly grinned. "Hell, no."

Chuckling, Harper glanced through an open window toward a large, kidney-shaped pool landscaped with tropical plants. Half of Pine Hills was here. Some guests splashed in the water, others relaxed beneath tables topped by beach umbrellas. Mirabella was in the pool perched on the shoulders of Ansel's cowhand, Jeff Davis, her enviably long, tanned legs dangling over his shoulders, her blond, feathered mane miraculously dry. Ansel Walters and Cam, both wearing white chef's aprons over their jeans, presided at the grill, while Blanche McCann, who'd just come down from the ranch house, fussed around setting out condiments on a picnic table.

Macon sighed. "She's convinced that if Cam so much as flips a burger he's going to die on the spot."

Harper frowned. "His trip to the hospital must have scared her."

"Something fierce," admitted Macon. "Scared me, too." Not that he seemed in the mood to talk about it. His eyes were skimming her swimsuit. "So, why are you really in the bathhouse, Harper?"

She lifted a stack of fresh white towels. "Our son sent me." *Our son*. It was the first time she'd said the words.

"Funny." Macon lifted two towels in a fisted hand. "He sent me, too."

"Must have forgotten he asked me to come?" suggested Harper.

Macon looked dubious. "I don't think so."

"Me, neither," she confessed, confused by Cordy's behavior. Her frown deepening, she dropped the stacked towels onto the sill, then leaned in the window, looking for Cordy in the crowd and feeling the light summer breeze caress her skin.

Macon looked puzzled. "What do you think he's up to?"

She shrugged, then tensed, fighting a shiver of awareness as Macon edged beside her, her next breath filling her lungs with the sun-warmed cocoa butter he'd so generously slathered on his skin. Her hair was swept into a sloppy chignon, and as his warm, taut belly grazed hers, he caught a stray wisp between his fingers, felt it a moment, then arranged it on her neck so seductively that she shivered.

He raised an eyebrow. "Cold?"

She couldn't fight the smile tugging at her lips. "Frigid."

He grinned. "Somehow, I doubt that, Harper."

She shrugged. "Covered with all that cocoa butter, you smell like a melting chocolate bar, you know."

Undisguised desire darkened his eyes. "But am I good enough to eat?"

Now, there was a pleasure they'd never shared, and

suddenly it seemed a crying shame they never would, at least not if he married one of his guests day after tomorrow. She'd like to feel his mouth...*there,* so warm and practiced. Imagining the touch of his tongue, she suddenly felt as if wine, not blood, was flowing through her veins. She swallowed hard, an unforgivably jagged pulse making that blood zigzag drunkenly to her every last nerve. What were they really doing here? Macon simply couldn't get married! Still inhaling cocoa butter, she detected another scent, one more powerful, more male.

As he edged closer, making sure the height of the window kept their lower bodies from prying eyes, she gasped. His damp trunks brushed her suit bottom, and she realized he was in a highly aroused state. "Good enough to eat?" she managed. "In just two short days, such questions will be better left to your wife."

Macon hardly looked in the mood for light sparring. His eyes still dark with male hunger, he gruffly said, "I'm awfully glad Cordy sent us to get these towels."

Relieved to hear his wedding seemed the furthest thing from his mind, Harper glanced away, through the window, just in time to see Cordy and Judith watching her and Macon. Cordy waved, then ran for the pool, leaping and wrapping his arms tightly around his drawn-up legs, doing a cannonball.

"He displaced half the water in the pool," remarked Macon.

"Right onto Mirabella's hair," Harper said with a laugh. Jeff Davis had ducked, too, playfully tossing Mirabella backward off his shoulders just as Cordy hit the water.

"I'm glad she's found another man to prey on," Macon admitted. "I can't imagine marrying her."

Harper sent him a long glance. "Too young for you?"

Macon tried to looked as if his male pride was ruffled. "There's no woman I couldn't take on," he promised. "But as long as it takes her to do her hair, she'd never be ready to get married by the end of this week."

Harper forced a smile, then wondered what was going on with Cordy. Was he worried about her? Was that why he was trying to throw her and Macon together? After all, Bruce was gone. She was alone. Maybe Cordy was concerned about how she'd feel two years from now, when he went away to college. Besides, Macon *was* his father. Did he feel his parents belonged together? "I don't know what brought this on, but I'll get to the bottom of it," she suddenly said, barely realizing it was a complete non sequitur. "Don't worry. Maybe it's only natural Cordy wants us to get together."

Macon murmured, "Right now, *I* want us to get together."

Now, yes. But what about later? Before she could ask, Macon had smoothed a hand over her hip. When it molded to her skintight suit, then slid over her backside, sweetly caressing her flesh, she decided she didn't care about later. She came to him like a bee to honey, with the fleeting, bold realization that the windowsill hid them from the crowd outside. No one could see....

When Macon's free hand glided down her bare belly and between her legs, she gasped, and when a thumb stretched, dipping and rubbing a deep warm circle into the crevice of her uppermost thigh, her inhalation was audible. Her flesh was swelling, aching inside her suit. "Macon," she murmured with need.

"Harper."

It would be so easy to let him keep touching her...to let go completely...to take the pleasure she'd wanted so badly last night up on Star Point, a pleasure she knew Macon could be so adept at providing. But their son—not to mention every prominent citizen in Pine Hills—was right outside! Suddenly, the humming chatter of conversation seemed deafening. Her urgent warning came out sounding hoarse, breathless. "Macon...no!"

"No?" Glancing up, she saw a naughty smile curving a kissable mouth that looked beyond irresistible. "I don't know about you," he whispered, his thumb brushing, then slowly stroking the front of her suit, the touch electrifying, the gentleness excruciating, her knees weakening as he slipped a finger under the leg band, "but I'm just in here looking for some towels, Harper."

Her heart was pounding, her limbs feverish with heat. Pure frustration claimed the rest of her. "There aren't any towels in my swimsuit, Macon," she whispered, her voice shaking.

"Are you sure?" he whispered back, shooting her a look of mock confusion as his hand gave up on the leg band of her swimsuit and headed southward, but only to dive once more under the elastic at her waist. Then a stroking, teasing finger was circling her folds, tangling in her curls, feeling so warm on her that she shivered again, her buttocks tensing. "Maybe you'd better just let me take a look," he whispered silkily against her ear.

She whimpered, the suit that was now pushed down around her thighs feeling suddenly too tight and constricting, since it forced her legs to stay pressed together when she so desperately needed to open them for him, especially when she felt his burgeoning erection nudge her thigh. She hoarsely whispered, "Look?"

"Yeah...look," he said raggedly, sending a searing gaze downward, where his finger slowly, deliberately parted her swollen, lush folds. "Pretty," he announced in a low growling whisper. "Sweet."

His magic touch caused her to whine, but through closed lips because she feared the extreme pleasure would make her cry out. Her heart hammered, and she glanced toward the pool. Just hearing the splashes increased her edginess—and her arousal. "Macon," she whispered breathlessly. "We can't..."

"We are."

"Someone will see us."

"You're going to come, Harper."

There was no fighting it. She was almost there already. Her fingers curled tightly around the window ledge, and even though everything in her warned against it, she took one last fleeting glance toward the pool, then gave in to the feeling. As she arched for him, her free hand sought his damp trunks, closing around where he was so rigid.

He groaned. A finger glided inside her, then another, and with every thick, mind-darkening thrust, she fantasized it was more...that it was the hard length of pulsing flesh along which she glided her hand. What were they doing? she wondered vaguely. With so many people nearby, this was simply too decadent. Too delicious, too. One touch, and jittery need had completely claimed them. Overpowered them. Devastated them.

There was nothing but the wonderful magic of his fingers, the torturous circling of a thumb around the love-slickened nub of her pleasure. Knowing she'd shriek, Harper bit down hard on her lower lip, tasting blood. "Dammit, Macon, they'll hear," she managed to whisper.

"Let them," he growled, his hips arching in time with hers, the once slow, controlled rhythmic dance of their hands breaking up, her fisted hand tightening around an explosive erection it could barely contain, his love-moistened fingers moving like quicksilver. His breath was a soft pant against her cheek when he whispered, "Now, Harper."

As if only his voice had touched her, she convulsed. Gasping, he climaxed with her. A few moments later, still wrapped in his embrace, she slowly came out of her sensual haze and became aware of the dampness of his trunks, the heat of skin warmed by sex, the hard hammering of his heart.

And then, just as suddenly as it had all begun, elastic snapped into place again. Harper jumped back. "Thanks, Macon! That hurt!"

"Sorry, but..." Macon was glaring toward the pool. He didn't blink. His eyes had gone flat and watchful behind the short, stubby fringes of his gold eyelashes.

Flustered by her ebbing arousal and half furious, Harper jerked her head to follow his gaze, gasping as Carrie Dawn burst through the crowd, rushing toward the bathhouse. "Something's wrong," Harper said, her heart still beating too hard as Macon edged protectively in front of her. "What's going on? Is somebody chasing her?"

Macon didn't move a muscle. "Wearing that," he muttered, "it's hard to say what Carrie Dawn's got on her tail."

Instinctively, Harper closed her fingers over his forearm, and a muscle twitched reflexively. Coarse hair rose on his smooth, corded skin, bristling the way hair did on the backs of wary cats. With a shudder, she glanced down. It was a good thing, she thought, a flush rising to her cheeks, that his trunks had been wet.

"There really isn't much to her suit," Harper managed to say nervously, coming to her senses and lifting her gaze, taking in the bright blue thong bottom clinging to Carrie Dawn's slender frame. The top was even skimpier. Her lower lip was thrust out, and a seeming gale force of furious sighs kept catching her jagged red bangs, blowing them upward on her forehead. "Mirabella's got on even less."

Without taking his eyes from Carrie Dawn, Macon said, "Really? I'll have to look."

Harper swatted him.

Without otherwise moving, he caught the open-handed blow. "C'mon," he said rhetorically. "Why do you think Carrie Dawn's coming this way?"

"To save you from murder?" Harper returned.

"That, or to interrupt the kiss you were about to get."

Harper's throat felt tight. "I was about to get a kiss?"

"Only if you said I looked good enough to eat."

"Anybody ever tell you you've got an ego the size of Texas?"

He didn't answer. His eyes were still locked on Carrie Dawn, and he looked worried, as if he were beginning to think she might be in need of rescue. The crowd had parted enough that Harper could see a man was chasing her. "Who's that?"

Macon shook his head. "Never seen him."

"He's not from around here," said Harper. "No Wranglers. No cowboy boots."

"No belt studded with turquoise," agreed Macon.

The middle-aged stranger was pleasantly pudgy, the open sides of his steel-gray suit flapping in the breeze, exposing a belly that tested the buttons of a summer-wilted button-down shirt. While his body wasn't about to win any contests, Harper could see a firm jaw and gentle gray eyes that hinted at possible good character. He looked furious, though, evidenced by how tightly he was clutching a briefcase, his knuckles turning pink, then white on the handle.

Macon whistled. "Wonder what Carrie Dawn did to him?"

"Aren't you going to rescue her?"

"Sure. When she gets here, I'll open the door for her."

"Well, maybe you're right," admitted Harper. "The way he's huffing and puffing, she'll definitely get here first, and as mad as he looks, maybe it's better if she locks herself in here with us."

The long, transparent, white blowsy cover-up that Lois Potts wore over her string bikini billowed as she ran to see the action. Cordy, Garrick, Jeff and Mirabella were fighting over a ladder, trying to get out of the pool. Cordy lunged out first, dripping wet, and raced worriedly after Carrie Dawn. Judith, who'd been relaxing under an umbrella with Chantal, rose and walked a few astonished steps in the grass, while Blanche McCann restrained her husband, no doubt terrified that whatever was about to happen would make his blood pressure soar. Anna and Diego had disappeared hours ago.

Carrie Dawn didn't make it to the bathhouse.

She was a scant five feet away when the stranger caught her upper arm, whirling her around. Just as Macon started for the door, Harper tightened her grip on him, holding him back. "No," she said, keeping her voice hushed, hoping the man wouldn't hear her. "I think it's all right."

The man heard her anyway. His dark eyes darted to the window, and he dropped Carrie Dawn's arm just long enough to stride over and grab a towel from the sill. Returning to Carrie Dawn, he thrust it at her. "Cover yourself," he commanded.

"Cover myself?" screeched Carrie Dawn, stomping a bare foot on the concrete patio. "I'll do no such thing! I'll have you know that some men think I look good this way, Charlie."

"Charlie?" murmured Harper. "Her boss from the Mountaineer Equipment Company?"

Charlie's voice was every bit as twangy as Carrie Dawn's, with not the syrupy, elongated vowels of the deep South, but angry, hard-edged consonants more akin to hill country. "I'll just bet they think you look good, little darlin'."

"Don't you dare call me your little darlin'!" she shouted. "You're not even my boyfriend anymore."

"Maybe not, but there's no way in hell you're marrying a man you don't even know!" roared Charlie.

"Getting married and helping to run a ranch would be better than sticking around West Virginia, in love with my boss," she said, fuming. "Don't you think so?" Before he could answer, she plowed on. "How do you think I feel, Charlie? Everybody in the parts and shipping departments knows the truth about us. So does every cook in the cafeteria."

"That's ridiculous! How could the cooks know?"

"Because before two months ago, I went down there every single day to have breakfast, and they know just how I like it. But now..."

Charlie merely stood there, his steely eyes wide as saucers. He dropped the briefcase he was clutching. It hit the grass with a thud. The towel followed. "Is there some reason you're not keeping down your breakfast, little darlin'? Is there something you're not telling me, Carrie Dawn? You'd best start talking right now!"

Carrie Dawn's mouth was clamped tightly shut. Harper had never seen such a look of helpless fury on a face, except on small children. Red bangs spiked into huge blue eyes that were flooding with tears the girl wouldn't let fall. Her chin quivered.

Charlie was staring at her hard. "Are you with child, Carrie Dawn?"

"I'll never trap any man into marrying me," she vowed.

"Oh, no, I've heard what you've done," he growled. Dropping to his knees and opening the briefcase, he lifted out a small black velvet box. "As if I'd let you marry a stranger, rather than me," Charlie continued, rising. "Ever since I heard the news, I've been trying to find this address. I called your folks and your sister."

Carrie Dawn was eyeing the ring box and blinking rapidly. Leaning, she daintily picked up the towel Charlie had let fall to the ground and contritely wrapped it around herself, knotting it tightly above her small breasts. Her voice turned as soft as water. "You swear? You really called my folks, Charlie?"

Taking a deep breath, Charlie tried to restore his dignity by tightening the knot of his tie. Everybody around them had gone quiet. Most were out of the pool, and Harper couldn't hear any splashing. Ansel suddenly seemed to remember himself, and looking torn, finally ran toward the grill to check on the hot dogs and hamburgers.

Charlie stared at the ground a long moment, and suddenly Harper felt for him. He was easily ten years Carrie Dawn's senior, but when he raised his gaze, she could see the love he felt for the volatile young woman. No doubt, having an affair with a girl from his office was the last thing he'd intended to do. His throat worked visibly as he swallowed. "I wanted what was best for you, little darlin'," he said. "You're still so young. You've got so many dreams, but I'm already settled."

Carrie Dawn's chin trembled. "But what if you're my dream, Charlie?"

Harper's eyes stung. "How sweet," she murmured.

"Are you pregnant?" Charlie asked brokenly.

Carrie Dawn nodded, tears falling. "I couldn't tell anybody. If I stayed at work, everybody would know it was your baby when I started to show. Oh, we never told anybody about our affair, but people guessed. And I can't have a baby without..."

"Having a papa for it?"

She nodded again.

Charlie's voice sounded strangled. "Then why did you come out here to marry a stranger? Did you fall in love with him through writing him letters?"

Carrie Dawn gasped, looking stricken. "No! I just wanted to make you jealous, Charlie!"

Her heart aching, Harper could almost feel the man's relief. He leaned so close to Carrie Dawn, whispering in her ear, that Harper didn't hear him propose. She saw the ring, though, probably more clearly than Carrie Dawn, since the other woman was crying so hard. Right after Charlie slipped it onto her finger, he draped an arm around her and led her toward the ranch house, looking for some privacy.

Harper had almost forgotten Macon was there until he murmured, "I'll be damned. I never knew you were sentimental, Harper."

Coming to her senses, she dragged a hand through her hair. "Sentimental?"

"Yeah." Drawing her into his embrace, Macon

brushed fallen strands of hair from her forehead, stroking a thumb beneath her eye to catch a tear.

"I'm fine," she protested as he brushed her other cheekbone, the touch slower and more tender than any she'd ever felt.

"No, you're not." His eyes fixed intently on hers. "Ever think of getting married again?"

It was the last thing she'd expected him to say. She couldn't breathe. Was he thinking about proposing to her instead of to one of his guests? Was he falling in love with her again? "Maybe," she ventured.

Pulling her closer, he fitted their hips together, making sweet heat flood her. "I'm not going to marry any of these women, Harper," he said, gazing down. "I thought about it last night, when we were up on Star Point. I don't know what's happening between us here, but maybe we can start getting to know each other again. Maybe we can...take it slow. Start going out some."

She almost laughed. That idea was unexpected, too, but he had her emotions so tangled up that she hadn't a clue what she felt anymore. *Start going out some?* She and Macon McCann probably wouldn't get past the nearest bedroom. Obviously, he wasn't thinking very clearly, and he seemed to have forgotten the whole reason he had to marry so quickly. "What about Cam?" she forced herself to say, not about to build false hope on the heat of the moment. "What about his health? He's had a stroke. Isn't that why you have to get married?"

Macon eyed her a long moment. "Cam," he finally said, with what might have been a trace of bitterness lacing his words. "Yes, I do have to think about Cam."

8

HOURS LATER, as he mulled over Cam's health, Harper's words were still in Macon's ears. Dammit, she'd almost sounded as if she *wanted* him to wind up married tomorrow. Since the conversation, he'd changed, pulling a worn, unbuttoned denim shirt over fresh jeans, and he glanced up sharply from where he'd been staring through the windows of the north wing study, into a night lit with floodlights and fireflies. "I thought I heard somebody come in," he said to Cordy, his heart tugging strangely as he watched his son drop into the brown leather armchair in front of an oak desk. "Where've you been?"

"Talking to your brides." Cordy was grinning and shirtless, still wearing his swim trunks, blond hanks of hair hanging rakishly into eyes the exact color of his mother's, and Macon was struck once more by how strongly he resembled Harper. Even now, it seemed impossible that this boy belonged to him.

"Everybody's gone now," Cordy added.

Was Harper? Macon wondered distractedly. As soon as they'd started talking about Macon getting married, she'd bolted from the bathhouse. He frowned. "Where's Charlie, Carrie Dawn's fiancé? Is he still here?"

"Out shopping for some Wranglers. Your Mom—er,

Grandma—put cots in her sewing room for him and Carrie Dawn. He only brought one extra suit, and Carrie Dawn wants to stay a few days." Cordy's smile broadened, his eyes glinting with boyish wickedness Macon didn't quite trust. "Carrie Dawn promised, no matter who you chose, Macon, that she'd be a bridesmaid, which is why she's staying, and why I'm here."

Amused, Macon arched an eyebrow. "You want to be a bridesmaid?"

Cordy scoffed. "You know that's not what I meant, Macon. Be serious. You promised you'd announce your engagement tomorrow—"

Macon couldn't completely disguise his foul mood. "That's not true. I didn't make any promises."

"Whatever," said Cordy, sounding unconcerned. "The whole town expects you to announce your engagement tomorrow, so I just came up to say I want you to marry Chantal Morris."

Macon nearly collapsed against the window frame. Leaning against it, he squinted hard at his son, staring in stupefaction, unable to believe any of this. With luck, he could pinch himself day after tomorrow and find out this had all been a bad dream. Hadn't Cordy even noticed that Macon and Harper had taken off together last night? Besides, Cordy himself had thrown them together at the pool party. "You want me to marry Chantal?"

Cordy nodded. "You're not in love with any of these women, right?"

"What do you think?" Macon looked sharply at his son. "I don't even know them. And I don't know what you're up to, either, Cordy—"

"Just hear me out." Cordy raised a staying hand, his expression sobering as he leaned anxiously forward in the armchair. "Mom was right. Whoever you choose will be my stepmother. She'll have tremendous influence on me in the future, so I should definitely have some say in who you marry, don't you agree?"

There was no arguing that, but the words sounded oddly rehearsed, which made Macon's frown deepen. He wasn't about to be verbally trapped by a sixteen-year-old, even if it was his own son. "Right," he said, quickly adding, "but that's hardly the point."

Cordy raced on. "Tomorrow, Mom's planned a breakfast buffet on the lawn. Everybody in Pine Hills is going to be here, and after we eat, you're supposed to announce your—"

"Engagement," Macon interjected, the word coming on a frustrated growl. "I'm well aware of that. Besides, you already mentioned it. But given the fact the *engagement* is to last twenty-four hours, only until the very next morning when I'm supposed to actually get married, I hardly think we can call it a real *engage*—"

"I like Judith a lot, too."

The way his son had blithely continued, cutting him off, left Macon gaping. He simply couldn't believe the turn this conversation was taking. "Judith, huh?" he asked dryly. "Not Mirabella?"

Cordy shrugged, eyebrows the exact ash color of Harper's knitting together, his expression perplexed as if he were seriously considering. "Mirabella's interested in Jeff Davis now," he said slowly. "You know, the hand who works for Ansel."

"What a shame." Macon couldn't help but say it.

"It is," agreed Cordy, either missing or ignoring Macon's sarcasm. "But I think it'll work out, 'cause Garrick overheard Ansel saying he means to make Jeff a cow boss, and Jeff wants lots of kids, which is Mirabella's top priority."

"That and her hair," Macon added acidly.

Cordy nodded absently. "Anyway, since Anna and Diego just got mar—"

"They got what?" Macon pushed himself from the window with a powerful shoulder and put his hands on his hips. This was not to be believed.

"Married," Cordy said smoothly, "just like you're about to, day after tomorrow. They snuck off and flew to Vegas last night."

Macon couldn't get his mind around it. "Diego's older than I am, and he still gets drunker than a skunk every Friday night in Big Grisly's Grill. He can be a lout and a womanizer, and Anna's—" Abruptly, Macon cut himself off.

"Gorgeous?"

There was no use denying it. Macon nodded curtly.

"But she needed a green card," Cordy continued. "All her sisters live in the U.S., and now she can, too. Besides, they just got back and Diego's following her around like a puppy dog. Somehow, I think a woman who looks like that can convince him to settle down, don't you?"

Macon could only shake his head. What was happening around this ranch? It was usually so peaceful, but ever since Harper wrote those letters, it was as if everybody had gone stark, raving mad. "So that's why

Diego was missing from the barn dance and the pool party," he muttered. Sighing, he repeated, "Vegas?"

"Yeah, and since you're buddies with Sheriff Brown, we're hoping you'll talk to him, and maybe he won't scrutinize Anna too carefully. Okay?"

"I can see you've got this all planned out." Macon chewed the inside of his cheek. He was definitely beginning to realize that his son had an agenda. It was true what people said—you had to watch these teenagers like a hawk. "But what about Judith?" Macon suddenly coaxed craftily, barely able to believe his so-called "brides" were finding partners when he wasn't. "Mirabella's interested in Jeff now, Anna's married Diego, and Carrie Dawn's engaged to Charlie, so you see, if I marry Chantal..."

Cordy looked genuinely worried. "I know," he said, tearing his teeth nervously into his thumbnail. "I don't know what to do about Judith. She's a nice lady. She's the one who kept all these women from killing each other. She makes sure that they don't leave their beds a mess, and that they clean up after themselves in the bathroom. She's a born mother."

Macon had been watching him carefully. "Like yours, huh?"

Cordy shrugged. "She's on my nerves less since I moved in with you, Macon."

Didn't the fool boy know his mama was terrified of losing him? And why was Cordy asking him to marry Chantal, when earlier today he'd been pushing Harper at Macon? This didn't make sense. "Look, Cordy." He forced himself to speak. "I agree. Your mother was right. She taught you good values, just like she's discussed with me, among them that people marry for love."

Cordy looked surprised. "Take a look at you. Obviously, they don't."

"Oh, yes, they do," countered Macon. "That's why I'm not really going through with this." He'd given it long, serious thought, and Harper *was* right. Macon couldn't live with himself if he was a bad influence on their son.

Cordy's jaw dropped. "But what about Cam's health?"

Macon sighed, not entirely comfortable with his decision. "My father's a big boy, Cordy."

Cordy looked stunned. "He's going to die, Macon! You *have* to get married! Day before yesterday, he had to be rushed to the hospital."

"Don't you think I know that?" Macon bit the words out, barely able to rein in his temper. Tomorrow morning this whole town—a town where he was born and bred and lived—expected him to announce his engagement. If he didn't, he'd be hurting his father. He just wished his son hadn't come in here. Without even knowing it, Cordy was playing devil's advocate, acting as the voice of Macon's conscience.

He blew out an infuriated sigh. It was tempting to propose to Harper, but he couldn't. They'd traversed too much territory together over the years, and Macon wasn't about to be rejected by her, not again. Oh, last night she'd claimed she felt rejected by him, but the truth was, people only saw what they wanted to. Years ago, Harper could've come closer to his truck and found out exactly what he and Lois Potts were doing.

Instead, she'd chosen to jump to conclusions. Not that she'd been too far off base, a little voice inside his head said.

"I want you to marry Chantal," Cordy repeated. "She has no money, nowhere to go. Her folks love her, but her getting pregnant shook them up, so right now, home isn't the best place for her. She's really smart, Macon," Cordy urged. "She wants to graduate, but if she goes home..."

"You don't think Chantal will finish high school?" Macon swallowed a curse, wishing his son wasn't pulling his heartstrings.

Seemingly oblivious, Cordy continued thoughtfully, "You wouldn't necessarily have to sleep with her. I mean, she *is* only seventeen, Macon. Just a few months older than me."

Macon stared. "You think I'd *sleep* with an underage girl?"

Cordy looked uncertain. "You *do* have a reputation."

One it was high time Macon corrected. "People might think I'm wild, Cordy, but it's not true. Years ago..." Macon paused, wondering how to continue. "Years ago, when I was interested in your mother, and after she married Bruce, well, I..." He took a deep breath, then exhaled slowly. "I guess I acted as if more went on than really did with other women, just to save my pride."

Cordy's lips parted in astonishment. "You were just trying to make my mom jealous?"

It wasn't what he'd said, not strictly, but Macon nodded.

"Hmm," said Cordy, rifling a hand through his hair.

"Well, that's a relief. Anyway, the past is past, and I really think you should marry Chantal."

Macon tried not to weaken. "I can't."

Cordy thrust out his lower lip belligerently. "It's the only thing I've ever asked you to do for me in my life!"

Cordy was pulling out strong-arm tactics, and Macon didn't much appreciate it. His tone was meant to imply that Macon had abandoned him, which he hadn't, but Macon wasn't about to rise to the bait until Cordy added, "Please, Dad..."

Dammit, Cordy had never called him that before. Macon's mouth went dry, and he began pacing in front of the window, all but cursing the day he was born. Cam's health would fail if Macon didn't marry somebody, and Chantal had nowhere to go. But why did this have to be the first favor Cordy had ever asked of Macon? And was Macon really fool enough to hurt his father and son by refusing to help Chantal—and all on the off chance that Harper might...what? Eventually go on a few dates with him?

He realized she was standing in the doorway. His breath caught as he took in the snug fit of her stone-washed jeans. As usual, her hair was sloppily upswept. Pale ash tendrils teased her neck, and a robin's-egg blue T-shirt made her eyes look bluer than the Western sky. Eyes, he realized, that were less foggy and more brilliant in color because they were flashing with fury. "How long have you been standing there, Harper?"

"Long enough to observe your deep thinking processes," she said coolly, staring past Cordy at him. "Don't let me interrupt you."

Macon's eyes narrowed. "What are you talking about?"

"I said don't let me stop you." She huffed. "Go ahead. Marry Chantal."

Macon snapped. He simply couldn't fight the uncanny, blatantly charged energy that always had them going head to head. "Fine," he retorted. "Maybe I will."

HARPER HAD NO RIGHT to be mad.

That's what Macon thought moments later, when he changed his mind and barreled after her. He'd make her see reason if it was the last thing he did. He stormed along the hallway, his powerful jean-clad legs taking the wooden stairs two at a time, his blue shirttails flapping in his wake, blowing away from his chest. Why couldn't Harper understand his dilemma? What Cordy said was true. By rights, Macon should marry since Cam's health was on the line, and Chantal was the neediest candidate. Judith was old enough to fend for herself. She was going through a rough time, but things would work out for her.

Reaching a foyer cluttered with saddles, bridles and jackets, Macon muttered, "My head feels like scrambled eggs." Moments ago, he'd been telling Cordy he couldn't marry, not even to help Cam. What had happened?

"Harper, that's what happened," Macon said, with a soft venomous drawl as he spied her walking toward her silver compact car. He came down the porch stairs. "Dammit, Harper, don't you walk away from me. You stop right there."

He was stunned to see her actually obey him, her already ramrod-straight back stiffening as her steps stilled. Then she wheeled around, blue eyes he'd seen so aroused with passion now shooting daggers. "Don't take that tone with me, Macon," she warned.

Gravel crunching under his boot heels, he strode across the driveway, halting in front of her as she leaned against the driver's side door. "You're the one who started this, Harper," he reminded her.

She glared at him, not even the freshly sunburned pink of her cheeks hiding how she'd paled with anger. "Started *what?*"

"You damn well know what."

Challenge glinted in her eyes. "You'd better enlighten me."

"Having these women come here, that's what," said Macon, edging closer, his voice lowered with scarcely suppressed fury. "You started this when you wrote to women who wanted to meet me, warning them about what kind of a man I was. Oh, maybe I sent these women tickets, but you teamed up with my mother and made sure they got rides from the airport and that a reverend was available and waiting, didn't you?"

"Guilty as charged. You know I did."

She didn't sound the least bit sorry, either. "Then why are you getting so riled up," he demanded harshly, his knowing, amber gaze flickering down, not sparing any inch of her, "when I'm doing nothing more than following through on the plans *you* set into motion?"

Unfortunately, she didn't even have the common

sense to blush at her own contradictions. "I'm not mad, Macon."

"Funny," he said, "because you're sure infuriating me." He swiftly grabbed her, curling his huge hands around her upper arms, leaving dangerous inches between them, a scant distance Macon was suddenly sorely tempted to close. "Am I going crazy here, Harper, or didn't we lie in the bed of my truck last night, up on Star Point, talking and looking at the stars? Didn't you kiss me good-night when I drove you back to your car?"

Her eyes widened, and for a minute she looked so startled and unaccountably innocent that he felt a hairbreadth away from throttling her. "Lord, Macon," she said, "what's that got to do with anything?"

"What's that got to do with anything?" His usual calm was long gone, and he almost sputtered the words. "I thought we were having a pretty good time up there."

"Fair," she said with a shrug, sending emotion racing through his veins with the headstrong speed of a hot-blooded thoroughbred.

"Fair?" he echoed thunderously, his eyes sparking with fire. "You call any part of this fair?" The next thing he knew, his fingers had tightened around her biceps. He yanked her flush against him, his groin engorging as her hips slammed his. The woman reacted to that, at least, he thought with satisfaction. Oh, she tried to hide her response, but the artery in her throat was wild, the sunburn on her cheeks no match for the scarlet flooding them. She wanted him. Why couldn't she admit it? Why wouldn't she ask him to call off his farce of a wedding? "You'd better tell me what you're thinking right now, Harper Moody!"

She looked livid and so outrageously sexy that Macon had the sudden urge to drape her across the hood of her car and ravish her there, like some kind of animal. Everybody at the ranch could look on, for all he cared. Vaguely, he was aware of upstairs windows opening—as if he hadn't just written a king's ransom of a check for the air-conditioning bill.

Her tone was so surly it could curl hair. "What I'm thinking? About what?"

About how my standing this close makes every inch of you tremble and come alive, Harper. "About my marriage."

"I'm thinking exactly what I did last week!" Harper exploded, writhing against him, her chest heaving as she tried unsuccessfully to wrench from his grasp. "You're out of your mind! Are you really going to marry a girl you don't even know? Are you truly prepared for an interracial relationship with a woman half your age?"

"I never knew you were prejudiced, Harper," he replied, the soft taunt baiting her. "Do you have something against interracial marriage?"

"No, as a matter of fact." With her pulse pounding and her ample chest heaving, she looked as if she couldn't decide whether to kiss or kill him. "Love's hard to come by in this world, if you ask me," she informed him. "Which means we each have an obligation to honor any that comes our way. But that's exactly my point. You're not in love with Chantal!"

"How can you profess to know what I feel?" he asked, suddenly wishing it wasn't so difficult to talk, that the sun-warmed scent of her—the shampoo and chlorine and just plain angry woman—hadn't stolen his breath. "Oh," he added, dropping his hold on her, "I see. You know who I love, just as you knew, years ago, that I wouldn't marry you, right, Harper? You know who I love, just as you knew I wouldn't be an appropriate father for my own son."

"Cordy's not the issue here."

"Then what is?"

She was fighting to control her shaking voice. "You can't get married. You don't love these women. You don't even know them. What right do you have to take a vulnerable, seventeen-year-old girl into your bed, Macon? And one who's pregnant!"

Pure, almost murderous fury coursed through him. Harper had known him for years! Didn't she think any better of him than that? "I have no intention of sleeping with Chantal." He ground the words out. "She's only seventeen and separated from her family for the very first time."

Harper shot him a knowing glance. "You're not going to sleep with your own *wife?*"

"No!"

"Now I *know* you've gone out of your mind, Macon," Harper chastised. "Unless you intended to marry that poor girl, then sleep around behind her back."

"I would never sleep around on my wife." His words were measured. "You'd better watch that tongue of yours, Harper."

She obviously didn't know what was good for her. She didn't even acknowledge the warning. "Have you

discussed this with Chantal?" she inquired. "Does she
know you're only using her, that you don't even intend
to make a real marriage of this—"

Macon cut her off. "She's the neediest of the
women."

"Needy?" Harper gasped. "She's got a family that
loves her, even if they're fighting right now. Do you really think you'll be helping a seventeen-year-old girl
by offering her a sham marriage?"

"I guess that's between Chantal and me."

Harper's jaw dropped, and her eyes darted around,
as if seeking support or escape, he wasn't sure which.
"Do you really expect me to believe you intend to
marry a woman without sleeping with her or sleeping
around on her?"

Macon couldn't help it. He was genuinely curious.
"Why's that so impossible to believe?"

Bubbling laughter he feared was touched by hysteria
rose in Harper's throat. "You? Celibate?" She stared at
him what seemed like a full moment, looking mock-
ingly disbelieving, then she suddenly turned with a
snort of derision, reaching for the door handle to her
car. Something inside him gave. If he wasn't careful,
Harper was going to walk out of his life. And laugh at
him as she did it!

"Yes, celibate." His tone was low, lethal. "Mind telling me what's so funny about that, Harper?" When she
turned toward him again, he realized the laughter
didn't meet her eyes.

"You couldn't be celibate for an afternoon," Harper
retorted, shaking her head, the movement only serving
to further dislodge stray wisps of hair he longed to

touch. One particularly wayward strand licked around a cheekbone, then traced her jaw, framing her face perfectly. "Have you forgotten how you came into my house, not a week ago," she demanded furiously, "and practically stripped me in my own hallway?" She looked outraged. "The hallway of *my house,* Macon!"

"Better than the yard," he growled, the sheer force of memory landing his hands where they'd been moments ago, locked tightly around her biceps. "And no, I haven't forgotten." Her eyes widened, and as his lips hovered over hers, the glittering challenge in her gaze made him want to show her who was boss. Once more, he yanked her close. This time, his mouth followed. Lips crushed lips, then his tongue thrust deep, finding and stroking the sharp tongue that had been so hellbent on distracting him for nearly half his lifetime. He was shocked to feel it, but Harper actually opened for him, offering her tongue to his suckling, using her own to parry back. He could feel a shudder ripple through her, and the tips of her breasts peaked. Nothing was between them but her cotton shirt and a bra that felt decidedly flimsy. He bit back a groan, and where he'd gotten so instantly hard, he could swear she was softening. Heat seeped through her clothes, sending fiery hot blood swirling where it most counted, arousing him almost painfully.

He wanted her, but he drew back, leaving her lips wet and swollen, her eyes glazed like warm sugar. He wasn't about to claim a woman who gave him such a hard time. His eyes riveted where she had the audacity to wipe away his kiss with the back of her hand. "I can't believe you just did that, Macon."

"And I can't believe you'd wipe a kiss from your mouth that you so obviously wanted."

"What I want's beside the point."

"Why's that?"

"Because, first thing tomorrow, you're apparently announcing your engagement to Chantal."

He'd had it. Harper had pushed him beyond what any man could reasonably bear. He stared at her a long moment, his eyes flickering to her chest where her arousal was plain. Suddenly wanting to hurt her, he said, "You're absolutely right, Harper. Good night, then. I'll see you in the morning when I announce my engagement."

And then he turned on his heel and strode to the house.

"ROMANTIC, isn't it?" The new schoolteacher, Betsy, excitedly seated herself next to Harper on one of the metal folding chairs arranged in front of the microphone. "Macon was so commendably brave to ask these women to come," Betsy chattered, as she spread a napkin in her lap and daintily nibbled a croissant. "But to announce the engagement publicly is really something, don't you think?" Not waiting for Harper to answer, Betsy wrenched around, watching people drift from a lace-covered buffet table to their seats. "Heavens, who thought of all this? It's lovely."

"I did," Harper said. She could barely stand to admit it. Having this bridal breakfast buffet had been her very own brainchild, but she'd never imagined things could get this far. Staring at the microphone, she felt sick. Positively sick. She slid her damp palms nervously down the navy polyester slacks of her postal uniform and wished she didn't have to go straight to work after this. Last night, when she'd gone to tell Macon the news about Anna and Diego's marriage, the last thing she'd expected was to find Macon worrying over his choice of a bride—not after the evening they'd spent at Star Point, not after he'd stood in the bathhouse only hours before, saying he wanted... Well, Macon had never clarified what exactly he wanted.

But he'd definitely said he was marrying Chantal.

Harper hadn't been about to let him see how the news affected her. It wasn't that she believed he'd really do it, but clearly he'd wanted to hurt her. And it had worked. She'd fled to a home that felt huge and empty and unwelcoming without Cordy. Even scary, since she was so used to having men in the house. Not that she could blame Macon for that. Cordy was bound to leave home soon, anyway. Besides, it had been fine to be alone last night, since she'd only flung herself on the bed and cried. Didn't Macon realize this was their only chance to be together? Why couldn't he see *her* as a possible mate?

He does, Harper, she assured herself. *He said he wanted to start dating. He's just toying with you. He won't really announce he's marrying Chantal.* But if he did... *He won't, Harper!* She shook her head to clear it of confusion. Should she stop him somehow?

How?

Panicked, Harper glanced around. Everything felt so off-kilter, so out of control. Even worse, Macon was right. *She'd* put this whole fiasco into motion, feeling sure Macon would have to confront the fact that he'd never settled down.

Her heart lurched. Macon was striding to the podium.

Just looking at him reminded her of how he'd kissed her last night, grabbing her and simply hauling her mouth to his, like some Neanderthal. She'd been livid, but she'd liked it, and the charged, passionate energy of that kiss made her shudder once more. If he said he was marrying Chantal, should she hop up and tell the crowd about that kiss?

Why not? she thought. *It'll be easy. Hop up, turn around, then calmly tell everyone Macon's been seeing you while he's been courting these women.* If that didn't work, maybe she could simply tell his female guests he was impotent.

Yes. Very calmly, she'd float to her feet and announce that Macon McCann suffered from erectile dysfunction.

What else could she do?

When he flashed a smile around the crowd and reached for the microphone, Harper pressed trembling fingers to her belly, feeling another wave of self-loathing. He looked better than ever, dressed in new jeans, a pressed white shirt and a Stetson. Her mind reeling, she barely felt her son's hand on her shoulder. "Mom?" he whispered from the seat behind her. "You okay?"

No, she wanted to scream. *You fixed your father up with Chantal Morris!* "Fine, Cordy," Harper said, sending him a smile. Was this really happening? she wondered, turning around. Why didn't somebody in this town put an end to these ridiculous events?

Surely, Macon would. Blowing out a sigh of relief, she told herself that's what his stern expression meant. Too bad he wasn't cutting to the chase. He avoided her eyes as he exchanged pleasantries with people in the front row, then thanked everyone for helping him welcome his guests to Pine Hills, then he announced Diego and Anna's marriage.

Finally, he leaned closer to the microphone and said, "It's been a long week, folks, but we've all started some new friendships. Maybe some—" he shot Mirabella and Jeff Davis a significant glance "—will turn out to be friendships that last a lifetime. We've gotten to know each other better, and I'm pleased to say I've met the woman I'm going to marry."

Now, Harper. Now! Leap up! Just start babbling about what's been going on between you and Macon. Her body froze, though, and the words lodged in her throat. Deep down, Macon knew how she felt about him, so he wouldn't marry someone else. Surely, he was going to do something incredibly sweet right now—like surprise her and tell the crowd *she* was the woman he wanted to marry.

Instead, Macon said, "I'll be marrying Chantal Morris tomorrow morning. Hope you'll all be there."

9

"YOU HAVE some nerve," Harper muttered that evening, standing stock-still in her kitchen, watching in undisguised shock as Macon strode down the hallway toward her. She was so stunned she temporarily forgot she was clad only in a short blue nightie with long, belled sleeves. Macon hadn't even bothered to knock.

He was dirty and sweaty, wearing dusty jeans he must have worked in today, a once-white T-shirt streaked with oil, its seams bursting at the shoulders—and yet he looked like heaven. Beneath the rough five o'clock stubble covering his jaw, she could see where his skin had taken on a reddish cast from new sun. Stopping, he crowded into a doorway that, for most men, would have been more than ample. He barely fit, of course, every troubling inch of him filling it as he wedged a powerful shoulder to the frame, stretching an arm like a sinuous jungle cat so he could rest a palm against the molding.

He looked at her in a way she could feel clear across the room, his penetrating eyes the warm color of honey in the lamp-lit dimness. He seemed bothersomely oblivious to her attire, taking in the red-and-white country decor instead, studying some festive tea towels she'd looped over cabinet knobs, then the black linoleum tile she'd laid herself. Didn't it bother him at all to see these things she'd shared with her husband? Harper wondered. Swallowing hard, she averted her gaze to the hot summer night through the screen door.

He finally drawled, "Going to attack me?"

She'd been trying to ignore his blatant perusal of her belongings. "What?"

"The spoon, Harper."

Quickly, she glanced down. Her fingers were gripped so tightly around the handle of a slotted spoon that her knuckles were white, and she was brandishing it, half raised, as though she meant to use it as a weapon. "You're not worth the bother," she assured him, feeling oddly unbalanced but pleased her voice didn't sound strained as she plopped the spoon onto a saucer next to where a pot of chicken vegetable soup simmered. Satisfied that she sounded merely angry, not hurt, or even worse, heartbroken, which was what she was, she did her best not to look too interested. "So, what brings you here, Macon?"

He continued leaning in the doorway, blocking her only exit. "If it's any consolation," he began, his assessing gaze reminding her of the thigh-high blue silk gown she wore, the scooped neckline of which suddenly felt scarcely adequate. "I've been sitting outside for a while, in your driveway, wondering the exact same thing."

"Consolation?" she echoed under her breath, hating that her traitorous attention had focused on the golden tufts of chest hair spilling from the neck of his shirt. "So that's why you're here? Do you actually have the nerve to come here and try to console me after your startling announcement this morning?" Beyond caring that he no longer seemed quite as unaware of her outfit, she rushed on. "Don't tell me you couldn't find something better to do with your last night as a free man, Macon? Shouldn't you be elsewhere? Maybe down at Big Grisly's Grill with Ansel and the hands, having some cute girl from Opossum Creek jump out of a cake or something?"

"Harper," he returned, seeming not the least bit affected by her sarcasm, "I don't think they do that at bachelor parties anymore. Men are a lot more civilized nowadays."

Laughter rose in her throat. "Doubtful," she announced, her slackening jaw communicating how ludicrous she thought *that* was. "Very doubtful. And you're some gentleman. You just stormed into my house without even knocking. Did you turn off your motor and coast down the road in neutral so I wouldn't hear you?"

It was barely perceptible, but she was pleased to see him color. "If I coasted—" his tone darkened "—maybe it was so, if I changed my mind and didn't come inside, I could more easily turn tail and run."

That's what she'd said he'd do at the altar. Was he mocking her? She couldn't help but say, "Coward."

"Look," he quickly added, "I'm here because my mother was worried about you."

And he wasn't, Harper supposed. "You didn't even knock."

"The screen door was unlocked."

"And that gives you licence to charge into my house?"

More than anything, she wished the grim set of his

lips didn't add to his appeal, making him look so formidably sexy. He drew a bolstering breath, suddenly frowned and said, "What are you cooking, anyway?"

She truly couldn't believe the non sequitur, but she realized that, with his intake of breath, he must have pulled in the scents of tomatoes, garlic, peppers and onions. Her eyes settled on him coldly. Had he forgotten he'd announced his marriage? "Nothing you're going to eat."

He almost smiled at the quick retort, and she couldn't blame him—it *was* clever—but damn him, how could he be amused under the circumstances? Even worse, her messed French twist was half undone, and she was sure he must have noticed her red-rimmed eyes by now. The last thing she wanted was for Macon to realize she'd spent the day crying over him. Just as she edged toward the sink—hardly wanting to know how disheveled she looked but nevertheless compelled to catch a surreptitious glimpse of herself in the toaster—Macon pushed himself off the door frame, helped himself to a pot holder and lifted the lid of the soup pot, swiftly leaning back to allow a rolling cloud of steam to escape.

He frowned. "Chicken vegetable soup? In summer?"

She stared at him. "I'm sick," she snapped.

"You don't look sick."

She fought the color rising to her cheeks. "Well, I am."

"Yeah, the post office said you left early today," he offered in a conversational tone that threatened to unhinge her, "and my mother said you dumped all the last-minute preparations for my wedding on her."

Helplessly, she watched him ladle out a cup of soup and rifle through drawers until he found a spoon. Not about to risk standing next to him, she fled for the stove, edging against it. Macon leaned against the counter opposite as if oblivious to her flight, blowing across the spoon before he took his first bite. For an instant, Harper was worried he wouldn't like it. She fought an impulse not to say, "Spicy enough, Macon?" Or, "Would you care for some pepper, Macon?" She hated herself for it. "What are you doing here?"

"Like I said, my mother sent me. She was worried. So is Cordy."

At the mention of Cordy, Harper's heart stretched to breaking. God, she missed him. "Since when did you ever listen to your mother?"

"Maybe contemplating marital bliss has softened me."

Harper very much doubted it. "I'm sure you have other things to do," she told him, watching him polish off the soup and feeling proud of the way she was getting her emotions under control, at least until he set the dirty cup in the sink where, she supposed, he meant for her to find and wash it. At that point, something perverse seized her. She'd never been this emotionally tangled up in her life. Houdini couldn't undo her.

He said, "What else should I be doing?"

Surely, he was intentionally prodding her toward fury. "Using your big, broad hands to tie all those little rice bags for tomorrow?" she suggested.

He crossed his arms. "Chantal offered to do it for me

so I could come over here and talk to you. I told her we had some unfinished business."

It was information Harper could do without. "Well, maybe you could pick up the cake," she suggested, crossing her arms—at least until she realized the movement made her hem rise dangerously close to the tops of her thighs. She dropped her arms. "Or why don't you make sure the musicians are lined up?" Inspiration suddenly hit. "Or you could take those flowers for the ends of the pews out of my refrigerator and to the ranch."

"Ah," he said, "so that's why you're making soup in this heat."

It was true. When the florist arrived, Harper had no choice but to use the vegetables so she could free refrigerator space for the flowers. "Just take them to the ranch, Macon."

"I get the distinct impression my wedding bothers you."

This time, she was adamant. "How could you even come here?"

"Easy. Got in my truck and drove." But he knew what she was really asking.

"Coasted in neutral," she corrected. "You've just told all of Pine Hills that you're getting married in less than twenty-four hours. I hardly think it's right for you to be calling on a lady friend, do you?"

"Is that what you are, Harper?"

"That, or the person about to get incarcerated for your murder," she muttered. Yes, the conversation had derailed, just as she'd known it would. It always did. Usually, the next thing that happened was that they made love. She edged another inch toward the stove, her eyes daring him to come near her and try anything funny. "If I ever was your lady friend, Macon, I won't be after tomorrow."

"If I'm getting married," he countered, "it's your fault."

"Big if. You announced it, didn't you? And it's not my fault. A woman can't force a man to marry a woman he doesn't love."

"You seem to have accomplished it."

"Why, then I must be a very talented woman."

"Very talented," Macon agreed, but this time an unmistakable innuendo and huskiness touched his voice, turning it so hoarse that Harper inched just another protective smidgen backward.

After a long moment, Macon added, "You're on fire."

"You're right about that, Macon." Harper suddenly fumed, every inch of her skin growing unaccountably warm. He'd hit the nail on the head. Truly, only *fiery* could describe how she felt. One day, Macon would probably make her implode. Or combust. Temper had warmed her, and she knew her eyes, red-rimmed from crying and raw from being rubbed with tissues, were flashing with heat.

"No, Harper," he said again. "I mean it. You're on fire."

"Fire?" she echoed and then, "fire! Oh, my God, I'm on fire!" Gasping, she leaped away from the stove, seeing yellow licks of flame dancing merrily along her belled sleeve. Lunging toward Macon and the sink as if she could outrun her own clothes and dive in a basin one-tenth her size, she cried, "Macon!" then turned in circles, but the movement fanned the flames. They shot upward, the silk as combustible as kindling, and she couldn't help but recall the fiery crash that took Bruce's life. Loosing a hoarse scream, she flailed her arm, flapping it against her side.

"Hold still," Macon commanded.

She spun instead, feeling the terrifying heat on her skin, then strong arms wrapping around her. Something thick and wet hit her sleeve, dousing it. Icy water splashed across her chest and hip, soaking her to the bone. Only then did she realize Macon had grabbed a dish towel dunked in frigid water. His hands roved over her, so sure, strong and protective that she was certain her heart would break from nothing more than the feel of them. She blinked rapidly, fighting tears. This was all his fault. If she hadn't been so desperate to escape him, she'd never have backed into the stove. *Just don't touch me, Macon. Don't hold me, not right now.* "I'm fine," she said, stepping back. "Really, I am. If you'll just go home, let me alone—"

"No, you're not fine, Harper." Swiftly, he pushed up her sleeve, pulling her arm to him and examining every inch of bare flesh, his eyes narrowed in concern until he seemed to accept the fact that, while her nightie was ruined, Harper wasn't even singed.

"If you want, we could bring in a microscope," she finally managed to say. "I think I saved Cordy's old chemistry set." The second the words were out, she wished she hadn't said them. Chemistry was the last thing she should be talking about with Macon.

Unfortunately, he looked intrigued. "A microscope?"

She nodded. "Just in case one of my hair follicles is still suffering from smoke inhalation."

When he glanced up from her arm smiling, she knew he was too close. Her heart was hammering wildly. Her breath was hampered. She told herself the cause was the accident, not his proximity, but she wasn't really sure. And maybe the truth didn't matter, anyway, not when heat every bit as dangerous as the fire was licking inside her, warming her as he gingerly pulled her charred, water-soaked sleeve down.

"I think you'll live," Macon pronounced, his eyes straying briefly to where silk clung to her drenched chest, and she colored, since there was no ignoring how the frigid water affected her. His voice was gruff. "You'd better go change, Harper."

Her throat felt raw. If Macon hadn't come here tonight, none of this would have happened. The way he was looking at her, she knew he was thinking about kissing her. Again. She knew she shouldn't let him, either. But was sixteen years of history between them really going to end this way? With her standing in her kitchen in a ruined nightgown while he was about to be married to a seventeen-year-old he didn't love? "Why are you here, Macon?" she asked once more. Had he come simply to torture her? In a near whisper, she added, "Is this some sort of payback because I didn't tell you about Cordy?"

He looked stunned. "No. Of course not."

She was on the verge of tears. "Then why are you here?"

"Because it's my last night as a single man, remember?" he drawled, sounding decisive, his amber eyes intent on hers, "which means I'd better start enjoying it."

SHE BLINKED. "Enjoying it?"

He nodded. "And for once, Harper, I plan to do so in a bed." Grabbing her hand, he wrapped his fingers tightly around hers, then turned and headed for the stairs. Thank God she followed, Macon thought with irony. He'd sure hate to have to drag her.

And drag her he would. Ever since he'd walked through the front door and glimpsed her in that short blue nightie, she'd been driving him mad with lust he couldn't fight. He still couldn't believe he'd announced he was marrying Chantal Morris, but that was exactly the kind of thing Harper drove him to. He wouldn't have done it, either, if he hadn't suspected that Chantal was changing her mind about getting married. Yes, Macon was beginning to suspect that his son and Chantal were matchmaking, trying to get him and Harper together.

Macon had only been to this house twice, never upstairs, and judging by Harper's silence, she wasn't in the mood to play tour guide. Macon found her room soon enough, anyway. His relief was almost palpable when he saw she'd probably redone it. Unlike those downstairs, this room held no traces of Bruce. No ghosts. No competition.

A pastel quilt covered the bed, and the brilliant yellow moon that had haunted Macon all week shined through fluttering dainty white eyelet curtains, the window open to the cooling night breeze. When they reached the bed, he turned to her with a surge of passion.

Moonlight did wonderful things to her skin, bathing it in gold, and her eyes were lit up with expectation, but her lips were pursed mutely, as if to say her ruined blue nightie offered substantive proof of some injury he'd done her. Some injury he'd done for years. His heart pulled. A good half of her *was* hopelessly, frigidly wet, and pride had her fighting not to shiver, even though her nipples had puckered so obviously beneath waterlogged silk. One sleeve was fine, the other in tatters, the burn holes in the fabric ringed by charred black circles.

"Harper—" he stepped close, cupping her chin "—I came to tell you I'm not going through with any of this. You know I wouldn't." Nothing could have pleased him more than the relief flooding her features.

She looked like she wanted to trust him—that was a start—and once more he cursed the lack of trust her mama had instilled in her. She said, "You're not? Really? You promise?"

He stared. Moonlight shone on her misty eyes, turning them the color of Star Point's lake at night, and he sighed, wanting her more than he ever had. "No. Of course I'm not." How could Harper even imagine it? Nevertheless, rifling a worried hand through his hair and glancing toward where the moon was framed in the window, he was hard-pressed to come up with any alternative plans. When he went back on his word, wouldn't his son feel betrayed? And if Chantal Morris didn't graduate from high school, Macon knew that would be on his conscience. Not to mention the failure of Cam's health.

Fortunately, one look at Harper drove those thoughts from his mind. "Now, c'mon," he found himself saying gently, "let's get this thing off you."

She'd gone strangely, uncharacteristically silent and was still staring at him, though her narrowed eyes were smoky and alluring. She sounded oddly disheartened. "This *thing?*"

This thing, just moments before, had been an incredibly enticing wisp of blue silk, tailor-made to drive a man out of his mind. It wasn't bad, even now, Macon decided, unable to tear his gaze from where it clung to her. The belled sleeves had been fit for a poetess, the neckline scooped and low, showing off the rounded swell of her breasts. "C'mon," he said, "let's get it off."

"You're just looking for an excuse to undress me, Macon," she whispered with mock petulance.

"The way you look right now," he admitted, glad her sassiness was returning, "I would gladly have lit the match that burned your clothes, Harper."

A pleased smile curled her lips. "How male."

"Not really," he whispered, edging yet another fraction closer, his fingers reaching down, lightly grasping the edges of a silk hem so short that it touched her panties. "In another minute or so, I'm going to show you how male."

"I'm waiting."

"And you'll keep waiting," he said with a smile, "since I mean to torture you all night long." His eyes never leaving hers, he pressed his palms to her sides, pushing the nightie up to reveal a skimpy blue silk triangle of lace panty that stole his breath, so transparent he could see the shadow of flattened, tangled curls. He was already stone hard, aching to be inside her, and he shuddered, his arousal strengthening as he pushed the wet, ruined silk over her ripe breasts. His palms dampened with the need to touch them, but he tossed away the gown, not allowing his hands what they wanted— no, he wouldn't, not yet. Thrusting his fingers into her hair, he reveled in the softness, easing out the pins.

"I can't believe it. After everything," she murmured as he arranged her falling hair around her shoulders.

She was so nearly naked, her breasts so full, the nipples so taut and pink. Barely able to think, he brushed his knuckles against her cheek, raggedly saying, "What are you talking about, Harper?"

"I can't believe that you're not getting married."

There was no use telling her he loved her. He'd learned that years ago. With any other woman, maybe that would work, but trust didn't come that easily to Harper. *Trust, dammit, that you abused.* Being young and dumb was no excuse. Macon's breath caught. "Do you really think I could marry one of those women?"

"You did put that ad in *Texas Men*," she reminded him. "That's why I wrote those women back."

"And I'm glad you did, since it got us together," he murmured, pulling her to his chest, leaning back just long enough to unbutton his shirt so she was snuggled tightly against his bare chest, his arm circling around her bare back, his skin tingling with the warmth and closeness. He sighed, sweeping his lips across the top of her head, the strands of her hair seeming like something precious. He shook his head. "What the hell have we been doing?"

She glanced up. "Torturing each other?"

He couldn't help but smile. "Somehow, I think we'll always do that, don't you, Harper?"

Her eyes captured his. "I hope so, Macon."

He did, too. And for the first time in years, he felt sure things would be fine between them. "Harper," he said simply, touching his lips to hers, feeling how perfectly they joined.

"What?"

He wanted to say this felt like the first time, maybe because they were going to make love in a bed, or maybe because he'd all but said she was the only woman he could marry. Instead, he deepened the kiss until the slow, languid touch of their tongues turned feverish. As he lost his mouth against hers, his hands found her breasts. Vaguely, he was aware she was trying to relieve him of his jeans, but he whispered, "No, Harper. I won't last."

Her tone was urgent. "I don't want you to last. I want you now."

"Then have me." Urging her onto the bed, taking in how the moonlight played on her nakedness, he said, "But I've been looking forward to this, so let's take it slow."

"I guess I could do that," she whispered.

Standing, his eyes fixed on hers, he slowly shrugged out of his shirt. Pausing, his hand on his belt buckle, his intent gaze swept down the only woman he'd ever really wanted, starting with where her head rested on a pillow, then taking in the ash hair curling on her shoulders, dropping to high, plump breasts outlined by where her swimsuit had been, the erect nipples the exact same sandy pink as her sunburn. Sucking a breath through clenched teeth, he tried not to linger on how those aroused tips would feel, moments from now, straining to his tongue. When his eyes dropped a final time, caressing a strip of panty barely covering her, he knew he wouldn't rest until his mouth was there and she was writhing beneath the heat of it.

He kicked off his boots, stepped from his jeans. Then he paused again, aware of the moonlit silence and how her eyes had riveted hungrily on the burgeoning arousal testing his briefs. Wincing against the pressure, he stripped them down, feeling so sensitive that nothing more than soft cotton made him gasp. Unbound, he was desperate to be inside her.

"Macon?" she whispered, her voice a croak.

He was thinking about how urgently they usually made love, in truck beds and back seats, on pine needles in the woods and in her hallway. He didn't trust his voice to be steady. "I've never made love to you properly, Harper."

Her eyes were half-lidded, glazed. "I wouldn't worry about being proper right now, Macon."

He wasn't, not really. "I meant in a bed, Harper."

He could see her throat working when she swallowed and the nervousness when she propped herself on her elbows. "I never saw you like this, either."

She meant she'd never seen him standing fully nude in front of her, so painfully engorged he wasn't even sure he could walk. "Then I won't move, Harper."

"But I want you to come here."

He released a rough chuckle. "Right now, I feel like I could—come right here, without moving." Instead, he leaned over the bed, catching her wrists and pushing them above her head, his searching gaze taking her in once more as he slid a hand between her thighs. She gasped into his mouth as he kissed her. And after his mouth found hers, it found her breasts.

Lower, beneath his cupped palm, beneath the scant barrier of soft silk panties, Harper was beyond damp and more than hot. Just like the sleeve of her ruined nightie, she was all wet fire, and he cupped her, using the varying weight and pressure of his palm until she was arching and twisting for it, his every shallow, panting breath bringing the aroused scent of her deeper into his lungs as he trailed blistering kisses from her breasts to her belly.

Slowly, he tongued her navel, and as he curled his fingers over the waistband of her panties, feelings so raw they had no name filled him. He eased the garment down. Watching the blue silk inch down her pink legs, he was beside himself. Feeling ruled by a power he didn't even know, he suddenly, impulsively looped the panties around her ankles—again and again—using the elastic waist and leg bands to bind her feet.

"Macon?" she whispered.

"Shush, now." Lifting her joined ankles off the mattress and using his head to part her knees, he came between her legs, letting the heels of her crossed feet settle between his shoulder blades. "I've never seen you lying down like this, Harper," he said raggedly.

She sounded faint. "I don't imagine so."

Beneath the hand splayed between her breasts, he

could feel the strong thudding of her heart. His own was hammering, his need for her so intense he wanted to beg to have it satisfied. His lips hovered over her navel. Only inches away, his thumb brushed open her cleft, then he leaned another fraction, his mouth covering her intimately, his mind reeling with her taste, his whole body spinning wildly with the musk of the kiss.

She twisted violently, but crazed with need, he wasn't to be robbed of a pleasure he'd dreamed about for years. He held her tightly so she couldn't escape the ministrations of his tongue, not its long straining strokes, nor the soothing pad of it, nor the flickering vibrations of its tip. Nothing could stop her from crying out in pleasured ecstasy when his palms glided beneath her, raising her to his mouth. Lips to lips. Fire to fire.

He gasped when her thighs quivered, shaking with the sweetest climax he'd ever felt. She pulsed to his tongue with a taste so shattering he couldn't last another second. He didn't intend to use a condom, either. He hoped Harper got pregnant again. They were still plenty young, and this time, Macon meant to be there when their baby was born...when he or she grew up.

But those thoughts weren't coherent. Macon was throbbing, barely able to think at all. Relief came only when he plunged into her. Silken and slick, she contracted around him, and her arms hugged him tight, every part of her taking him deeper. She clung, the heels of her bound feet pressuring his back while he plowed to her womb, loving her with everything he had.

His release was total. It emptied him, leaving him crushed and oddly vulnerable and yet feeling, somehow, like a new man. Touching her womb, coming with her, moaning their pleasure, he knew this was the end of sixteen years of crazy history with this woman.

Starting now, he and Harper were going to act sane.

10

NEAR DAWN, she and Macon shared a scented bath, so Harper woke smelling fresh as a greenhouse. Scarcely able to believe how thoroughly he'd loved her, she slid lower under the sheet, smiling into the pillow, still feeling half lost in dreams and never wanting to open her eyes. When she did, she saw bright, slanting rays of sunlight slicing through the thick leaves of trees and fluttering curtains. On a brief moment's panic, she thought, *I've slept too long! The sun's too hot and high in the sky!*

Her eyes narrowing, she quickly rolled over, but instead of Macon, she found a note: *I went to the church.*

Simple and straight to the point, it was scribbled on the back of an envelope and resting against a pillow in which she could still see the depression left by Macon's head.

Twenty-five to ten! she thought, her eyes darting to a clock. Macon was getting married at ten! Bolting upright, feeling as if an outside force was propelling her, Harper jumped nude from the bed, a voice inside her arguing, *He's calling off the wedding, that's all, Harper.* Hadn't she heard a word he'd said last night?

But what if he's not? Grabbing a terry robe, the first item she reached, she pulled it on, knotting the sash. No, she thought, striding into the hallway, if he'd meant to cancel the wedding, he'd have done so already, wouldn't he? She should have known! Everything was starting to make vicious, dreadful sense. Because Harper had written all those women, Macon had given her his final communication in letter form. No, he'd never hurt Chantal Morris. He wouldn't let her undergo the humiliation of getting up today, getting dressed and going to the church. Besides, if he *had* put off telling Chantal and was going to the church to do so, he'd have awakened Harper to tell her, wouldn't he?

Be calm, she commanded herself. *No matter what happens, he's Cordy's father.* But how could she be calm when this confirmed every dark suspicion that was her mama's legacy? How could she be calm when last night's lovemaking seemed to prove yet another time that she and Macon belonged together?

Pausing, Harper considered doing exactly what her mama had always wanted to do—pack and flee this backwater. She'd been a fool to stay after her husband died! And yet how could she have left a town to which Macon McCann always returned? *He's the richest boy in this town, young missy. Don't you be fooling yourself. He'll take what boys want, and then where will you be?*

Last night, Harper thought ruefully, he'd definitely taken what boys want. And today, she was exactly where her mother said she'd be—alone. From the front door, she stared into a morning so brilliant it hurt her eyes. Under the willow tree, where Macon's truck had been, the grass was brown, dryer than elsewhere in the yard, untouched by the sprinkler.

He was really gone.

How much time passed before she heard the motor? Her heart skipped a beat. Was it Macon? Was he coming back? With the possibility, relief flooded her, especially when she glimpsed snatches of red, the color of Macon's truck, flitting through the trees.

It was a compact, though, shooting down the road like a bullet. No, not a compact, a sports car—and the only foreign-made convertible in Pine Hills. "Oh, no," Harper groaned. "Not now."

But Lois Potts was zipping under the willow, parking where Harper had hoped Macon's truck would be, getting out without turning off the motor, tossing her cell phone to the seat, then jogging toward the porch. Even worse, Lois was dressed—as all Pine Hills was, no doubt—for Macon's wedding. Transparent, powder-blue layers swirled over Lois's knee-length sheath, her high heels sinking in a yard left soggy by the sprinkler. One manicured, diamond-besparkled hand clutched a shoulder bag so it wouldn't bang her thigh; the other was planted atop a straw hat, the brim of which was tied with a sash that matched the dress. "If the hat didn't blow off in your convertible, Lois," Harper whispered dryly, "it probably won't now."

And yet as she watched Lois loping toward her, a strange mixture of sadness, longing and nostalgia twisted inside Harper. From here, the other woman looked as young and vibrant as she had years ago. Dammit, why hadn't Harper had the nerve to look inside Macon's truck, to see what he and Lois were really doing? "You were too afraid to know the truth," she murmured, taking a deep breath as she stepped through a crack in the door. Oh, she was cordial enough to Lois Potts in the post office—the customer was always right—but she and Lois had never socialized.

Nor was Harper inclined to start now. She braced herself, feeling her knees weaken with panic as she shot a glance toward the kitchen clock. Eighteen to ten! Macon couldn't marry Chantal!

"Well, Harper," Lois began breathlessly, not wasting her time, "I heard Macon stayed here last night."

It was the last thing Harper expected, and she gasped. "The company I keep is none of your business, Lois Potts," she said indignantly.

Not to be deterred, Lois rushed on. "Don't pretend you don't know what I'm talking about, Harper. His truck passed Nancy's house last night at seven-oh-four. He was driving in neutral, and Nancy knew the exact time because, just as Macon passed, the timer for her poached egg rang. Betsy, Mary Sue and Penny saw him, too. Betsy was visiting Mary Sue, who was weeding around those prize irises of hers—you probably already heard she won another blue ribbon in Opossum Creek last week—well, anyway, Penny was hanging out laundry, you know how her kids run through clothes."

Nancy was Nancy Ludell, the notorious gossip at the end of Harper's road; Mary Sue lived in the house closest to Harper's. Glancing over her shoulder again, Harper's heart hammered. Fifteen minutes until Macon was married! "Your point?"

"Macon spent the night here last night," repeated Lois.

"Now, there's some real detective work for you,"

Harper said. "Maybe you, Nancy, Betsy and Mary Sue should all consider applying for work with Sheriff Brown."

"Maybe, but I wanted to speak to you because—" Lois began.

"Lois," she interrupted, "nothing personal. I didn't mean to be rude, but you've caught me at a bad time, a very bad time. I just got out of bed and—"

"Betsy just called my cell phone to say Macon's shown up at the church!" Lois protested. "Look, Harper, you don't like me, and I don't blame you. Because you got double promoted when you were a kid, you were younger than everybody else in our class, and I was, well…"

One of those girls who'd managed to be as loose as ribbons the day after Christmas, and yet just as popular. Lois had been the richest, the prettiest, the first girl to have breasts. "Really, Lois, it's just a bad time…"

Resolute, Lois tossed her head, her permed hair springing to action, tracing a determined jawline as she nervously gripped the shoulder strap to her bag. "Please Harper, things aren't how they used to be, you know, back in high school."

Definitely not, although Harper would never hurt Lois by speaking the truth, the way she imagined Lois was trying to hurt her now. Everybody in town knew Lois had divorced Jimmy Weston, the ex-captain of the football team, after he'd been caught in flagrante with one of their baby-sitters. As soon as the girl was seventeen, he got permission from her parents, married her and moved to Opossum Creek. Precious minutes were ticking away, but Harper forced herself to gentle her voice. "No, they're not the same, Lois." Her mind suddenly flashing on the time she'd spent with Macon on Star Point, Harper thought she'd cry.

Lois was biting her lower lip. "I saw you that night, Harper."

There was no doubt in Harper's mind about which night Lois was referring to. If so, it was the last thing she wanted to discuss right now. Hoping she was wrong, she said, "What night?"

"You know what night. Macon showed up at Big Grisly's Grill, had a few too many in the parking lot, and I all but dragged him to his truck." An obviously difficult admission, given the sudden downward cast of Lois's eyes, not that Harper was inclined to feel much sympathy. "Believe it or not, I always wanted to go out with Macon, Harper."

It couldn't be clearer if you were wearing a blinking neon sign. Harper made a diplomatically noncommittal humming sound.

"What I'm trying to say is that while Macon and I were making out, I saw you over his shoulder. I knew he was supposed to run away with you that night—I think I'm the only other person in town who ever knew. He told me. He thought you'd stood him up, and when I saw you standing on the edges of the parking lot, staring at us..." Her eyes met Harper's, begging forgiveness. "I never told him you came. I let him keep thinking you'd stood him up."

Flashes of that long-ago moonlit summer night, so like the nights this week, came to her mind—the horrible screaming match with her mama, how she'd brushed past her to go find Macon. Harper had been so full of dreams that night. Macon was going to take her away from it all.

"I appreciate your saying so," Harper said, angry and yet touched by Lois's gesture. "But I've told Macon myself. It wouldn't have made a difference."

"Maybe...but that night he showed me the prettiest diamond ring I've ever seen, Harper. He'd worked for Cam, earning the money for it, and he was going to propose to you. He told me so."

Harper's knees locked against the sudden stab of emotion. Macon was going to propose to her? Without even knowing she was pregnant with his child? She could only stare at the other woman, who was showing her age more than Harper, her eyes drawn at the corners with the tensions of single motherhood and of not fulfilling whatever expectations came with having had a young life brimming with opportunities, a kind of life Harper had known nothing about.

"Everything changed for me when Jimmy left," Lois added, her voice strained. "I still can't get my life back together, Harper. I know what love can do to a person. I didn't know that in high school." She paused, swallowing hard. "I'm the last person you want to hear it from, but Macon loves you. I don't know why you two never got together, but rumor has it Cordy's his boy. Anyway, Macon loved you then, Harper. And if he stayed last night, my guess is he loves you still."

If only Lois wasn't so dead wrong. "If you haven't noticed, he invited five women here this week so he could choose a bride, and now he's at the church." Harper's tone suddenly went cold, and as she glanced over her shoulder at the clock, despair gripped her.

Thanks for stopping by sixteen years too late, she wanted to say. "Lois, please. I appreciate it, but it's best if you just leave. He'll be married in ten minutes."

Lois Potts's chin went up, making her look every bit the snobbish girl she'd once been. "I was trying to be nice! Since Jimmy left me, I've been seeing a therapist over in Opossum Creek, and this was part of my therapy."

She wheeled around, and layers of powder blue swirled as she charged down the porch steps, across the grass, hopped into her sports car and slammed the door. Right before she drove off, she yelled, "If you don't wake up, Harper, you're going to wind up a total mess, just like me!"

MACON TRIED finding Chantal at the ranch, but everybody had left for the church. Hadn't they even stopped to worry over the whereabouts of the groom? Cursing soundly, Macon realized he could hardly show up at the service in the oil-soaked T-shirt and dusty jeans he'd worn to Harper's last night, so even though there wasn't time to shave, he quickly changed into the logical thing, the tux laid out for him, then he ran for his truck and sped toward the church.

The organ was playing. Folks from Pine Hills and Opossum Creek, all wearing their Sunday best, were crowded into pews, most fanning themselves since the weather was hot. So many flowers spilled from urns at the altar that Macon couldn't imagine any were still in Harper's refrigerator. The whole place smelled like a perfume counter. But no one would let him see Chantal. "What do you mean, I can't see her?" he growled at his mother.

"Seeing the bride in her wedding gown is bad luck," Blanche told him firmly, seemingly anxious to see her son married today so his father would retire. Pressing a hand to her heart, she rushed on. "Thank heavens you're finally here. We were starting to worry." Macon slipped away just as she turned to someone else, saying, "He's here. We can start."

While ushers and bridesmaids began marching, Macon slowly strode the hallways, peering inside Sunday school classrooms and offices. Chantal had to be here somewhere. Ever since Cordy had come to him, asking him to marry Chantal, Macon had been suspicious, sure she and Cordy were matchmaking. But what if he was wrong? Chantal had to be the first to know. He owed her that. Especially since, sometime last night, her extended family had flown in from Missouri for the wedding. Wincing, hoping he wasn't about to embarrass Chantal, Macon paused, glancing through a side door toward the two front pews occupied by Chantal's relatives. Macon couldn't identify her father, but a woman who was probably her mother looked confused and worried, wringing her hands and fanning herself with a wedding program as if she felt faint. Yes, Chantal definitely had to have a say in how things proceeded from here. Macon had complicated her young life enough.

But where was she?

He was still wondering when his mother grabbed his arm and forcibly pushed him through the side door toward the altar, saying in a hushed tone, "It's time, Macon."

Wearing the tux and facing the congregation, he felt like the worst kind of fraud. Strangely, no one lining the altar rail offered so much as a smile of encouragement—not Mirabella and Jeff, nor Anna and Diego, nor Carrie Dawn and Charlie, nor Judith and Cordy. Not that it mattered. Macon realized then, however unfortunate, the only way to reach the bride was to wait for her to walk down the aisle.

Surely, Chantal would come to her senses, anyway, if she'd really intended to march. Surely, she and Cordy had been matchmaking, trying to force Macon into Harper's arms. No, Chantal wouldn't really do this.

But she was. Once Macon sidled next to Cordy, the organ crashed thunderously, and Chantal Morris was taking measured steps toward Macon, the skirt of a tea-length white dress flowing over an ample midriff. Her veil was as long as the dress, the lace thick by her face, thinning as it fell. One hand held a cascade of daisies, the other clutched the stiffly held arm of a tall, thin-boned black man with austere, righteous features.

So this would be my father-in-law, thought Macon as they reached the altar. Not that Mr. Morris so much as looked Macon's way as he left his daughter and walked to the nearest pew, seating himself beside his wife, his averted eyes seething with emotion, his lips grimly pursed.

It was Macon's only chance. Just as Reverend Shute arrived in front of them, Macon leaned close. "Chantal, we've got to talk."

"Macon." Reverend Shute reprimanded him under his breath, his lips moving less than those of a professional ventriloquist, the blue eyes that sparkled when he was fishing with Cam radiating a solemnity he reserved for the pulpit. Thick silver hair, thrust back from his forehead, made him look unusually severe.

Vaguely, Macon was aware his son was staring between him and Chantal, looking every bit as worried as the Morrises. Chantal's face was covered, so Macon couldn't make out her eyes, much less their expression. Ignoring the reverend, he once more whispered, "Chantal?"

Reverend Shute only seemed to take Macon's urgent tone as his cue to rush into the ceremony. "Dearly beloved," he began.

"I've got to talk to Chantal," whispered Macon.

"We are gathered here today..." Reverend Shute paused dramatically, raising the prayer book from which he was reading in front of his lips in such a practiced way that Macon concluded he'd used this tactic before, and then he growled for Macon's ears only, "Cam's sick. He's had a stroke. You hear me, Macon? My best fishing buddy's health is on the line, and if you've got to be married today to take over that ranch, then married you'll be. Besides, don't forget, you *are* doing right by this sweet young woman, not to mention restoring a lot of faith in the power of love in this parish." Without missing a beat, the reverend lowered the prayer book, smiled and continued. "Gathered here, in the presence of this man, this woman and God..."

His mind reeling, Macon realized he was in a world

of trouble now. As if to prove it, Reverend Shute jumped from the preamble right to the vows. "You can't do this," Macon whispered, unable to believe what was happening. He had to stop the wedding. But how could he do so without embarrassing Chantal?

The prayer book had gone up again. "I have a feeling God's on my side," assured Reverend Shute from behind it. Lowering the book, he smiled benevolently at Macon and Chantal, then continued in a melodious bass, "Do you, Chantal Morris, take this man, Macon McCann, to be your lawfully wedded husband, to have and to hold, for richer, for poorer, until death do you part?"

Chantal's hands were so tightly wrapped around the daisy bouquet that her fingernails had turned bright pink. Suddenly, she tossed back her veil, turning to Macon. "I can't marry you. I can't!" she exclaimed, her facial color darkening, her pleading brown eyes darting around a crowded roomful of people, most of whom she'd never even met.

He registered the fact that she was beautiful—her coiled hair exotic under the veil, her light makeup bringing out the best in her features—and then he realized her guilt-ridden voice was gaining momentum, the emotional tone high-pitched. "I've been thinking, Macon," she said, "and since I'm having a baby, the most important thing for me is to finish high school. And we're not in love, Macon. Anyway, if you ask me, I've been bothered enough by boys for the moment. I need to be thinking about my baby and my high school diploma, and that's plenty."

Relief flooded Macon, and strangely, pride. Looking

at her, his gaze warmed. Chantal Morris was so fine. Young, strong and brave, wanting what was best for herself and her baby, just as Harper must have years ago.

"I can't believe my family came," she continued, her eyes filling with tears. "But one of my uncles—he's in the second row—well, he owns a shoe repair shop in Memphis, and when he heard the news, he got everybody plane tickets." A tear splashing down her cheek, she nervously picked at one of the daisies in her bouquet, pulling off the petals.

"Of course we came, baby," a female voice called, probably her mother, though Macon didn't know, since he couldn't tear his gaze away from the compelling dark eyes holding him.

"My mama and daddy love me, Macon."

"Yeah." Just as he loved Cordy and Harper. "Of course they do, Chantal." Macon knew that now.

"When they got here last night, I was so surprised, and then we all started talking. Judith wants to stay out here and try a new kind of life. And Cordy introduced me to some of his friends at the pool party. I think...if I just get away from my old friends, and my uncle subsidizes me a little, which he says he will, then maybe I can stay here and share a place with Judith. My folks took to her right off, and she's willing to watch out for me, at least until I graduate."

"Oh, hallelujah," sighed Mrs. Morris, pressing a hand to her forehead, then fanning herself madly with the wedding program. "Thank you, Jesus."

"Hattie, calm down," Mr. Morris said stoically, patting his wife's arm. "We knew Chantal would come to her senses. She always does. She's a good girl and we have faith in her."

Macon's breath caught at the sheer simplicity of the plan. Chantal had made fast friends with Cordy, and Cordy was popular, so that friendship would ease Chantal's way in a new school, despite that she'd be a senior, raising a baby.

But, even now, Chantal didn't look completely satisfied. "Macon, I'm sorry," she continued. "We shouldn't have let things go on this long, but your son thought if he begged you to marry me that—"

Macon glanced at Cordy. He'd known the boy was up to no good. "That what?"

Looking nervous and more dashing than most gangly teenage boys would in a tuxedo, Cordy said, "That you'd realize you love Mom." He frowned. "Is it true? Do you, Macon?"

Macon suddenly felt downright misty. "Yeah," he said. "I do. Truth is, Chantal, you don't have to feel the least bit bad about any of this. I was trying to find you to tell you we shouldn't go through with it."

"But they wouldn't let you see me because I was in the wedding gown," Chantal said, the realization hitting.

"Exactly," returned Macon, sighing with relief as he turned toward Cordy again. "Do I love your mother? I've been in love with her since the first time I laid eyes on her, Cordy. I'd marry her in a heartbeat if she'd have me."

"THEN STAY right there, Macon."

Harper, who'd been standing at the back of the

church, heard everything. Lois's parting words had had their effect. Feeling as if she'd been struck by lightning, Harper had raced upstairs, grabbed the first dress she could lay her hands on, which just happened to be the freshly laundered white sundress printed with bluebonnets Macon liked so well. She'd thrown it over her head, shoved her feet into shoes and run for her car, not about to make the mistake she had sixteen years ago and assume she knew the truth about Macon's motives, not without finding out the actual truth for herself. After all, the man had once intended to propose to her!

Of course, for one dismayed moment she'd stood there, registering Chantal's dress and Macon's tux, but then she would never believe he loved another woman until he looked her right in the eyes and said it. She wouldn't even believe it if he was giving every appearance of marrying Chantal Morris. With relief, she'd watched as Chantal threw back her veil and called off the wedding.

And then Macon had said he loved Harper.

"Harper," he drawled, surveying her from the other end of the aisle.

"I love you," Harper assured him, and strode down the aisle. She heard Lois Potts release a loud, racking sob, and from the corner of her eye, Harper saw her dab furiously at her patrician nose with a tissue, her wide-brimmed hat bobbing and nearly obscuring the weathered old face of Doc Dickens, a man who'd been Harper's doctor for years and who'd delivered Cordy. Cam and Blanche were in the front row, opposite the Morrises, who were all gaping at Harper as if to say nothing this strange had ever happened in the state of Missouri.

Harper rushed right into Macon's embrace and looped her arms tightly around his neck, hugging him tight, his pressed shirt and stubbled jaw feeling gloriously rough against her skin. She whispered, "Lois Potts came over this morning, and she said, years ago, you were going to marry me."

Macon leaned back a fraction. "I was. I am."

Her heart squeezed so tightly she could barely breathe. "Why didn't you ever tell me, Macon?"

His gaze was wistful. "Would you have believed me, Harper? Trusted me?"

"No," she admitted, her eyes stinging with the sad truth of it. She shook her head, knowing it wasn't his fault. "But I do now."

Her eyes never leaving his, Harper heard Reverend Shute addressing the crowd. "Sorry, folks, but it looks as if today's wedding's canceled."

"Oh, no," Harper said under her breath, not relinquishing her hold on Macon. "Doc Dickens is here, and I'm sure he can arrange blood tests, but right now, I want go through with this ceremony." She offered a watery smile. "It'll be a day to remember."

"Oh, really?" A twinkle crept into the reverend's eyes as if he'd known this would happen all along. "Fine," he said with a low chuckle. "Long as this boy marries somebody, Harper. It's time for him to take over the ranch now, and I tell you, those trout just don't bite if Cam McCann's not in my boat."

Still watching Macon, Harper grinned, and then she tilted her chin upward, her mouth finding his.

"That comes after the vows," murmured the reverend.

But the kiss only deepened, and Harper thought, *Step back. Let Reverend Shute do his work.* And yet she couldn't, not when Macon felt so warm and good, not when this kiss was showing folks in Pine Hills what they'd probably really known all along, that she and Macon loved each other to the depths of their souls. Finally leaning back, she huskily whispered, "You'll really marry me, Macon?"

He grinned, his amber eyes brimming with heat, gentleness and love for her. "Wild horses couldn't drag me away from this altar," he assured her with a slow drawl. "So, let's get to it, Harper."

"Yes," she whispered. "Let's get to it."

____Epilogue____

Six months later

"LIKE, YOU'RE NOT going to believe this," said Mirabella, "but it's another bag of letters, and they're all for Lois."

Harper grinned. After the wedding, Harper had wound up thanking Lois Potts for her visit, and not long after that, inspired by Macon's ad in *Texas Men*, Lois had begun advertising for a husband. Feeling glad responses were pouring in, but suddenly sensing something amiss, Harper glanced up from the sorting bin. Sure enough, Mirabella was hauling the mailbag across the lobby by herself. "Be careful," Harper warned, "Doc Dickens told you not to strain yourself, Mirabella."

Mirabella tossed a head of hair currently showing two-inch roots and paused beside the bag, smiling and running a hand over her swelling belly. "Why can't people give birth like insects?"

Harper laughed. "Insects?"

"You know," said Mirabella, "with a twenty-four-hour gestation period."

"I hear you," returned Harper, sighing because every day of her own six months were showing. Cordy simply couldn't believe he was finally getting a sibling, and raising this child with Macon was a dream come true. Harper felt content to draw out the pregnancy, savoring it.

But Mirabella was anxious. Three months along and married to Jeff Davis, she'd taken the job at the post office to avoid working with hair chemicals during her pregnancy. Besides, from the post office, she could watch the carpenters in the shop across South Dallas Street, just next to Happy Licks. Mirabella's L.A. Styles Salon would open there soon, and folks would no longer have to drive to Opossum Creek to get their hair styled.

Judith and Chantal had settled in the old Moody house, since Harper couldn't bear to sell a house she'd lived in so long and that had been so important to Bruce and his family. With Cam and Blanche McCann relaxing in Acapulco, Macon was needed at the ranch, and truth be told, Cordy hadn't wanted to give up a house with horses and a swimming pool. Diego couldn't be counted on to take up the slack. He had a headful of stars—as if America's newest citizen, the beautiful Anna Gonzales, had hit him with a skillet, instead of married him.

Harper's old house was also fast becoming a home office for the battered women's shelter Judith was opening. Otherwise, Judith was busy, while Chantal was at school, with Evan Eldorado Morris. He had been named after Chantal's father, and even though he'd been seven pounds at birth, he was quickly becoming more than a handful. All Chantal's teachers agreed she was smart as a whip and might get some scholarship money to attend the community college in

Opossum Creek, but if not, Cordy planned to squeeze her generous uncle for tuition.

Harper began sorting the mail again. "Oh, look, it's a postcard from Carrie Dawn!" she called excitedly, just as Macon breezed through the door. Seeing him, Harper suddenly frowned. He'd come from the ranch, grimy and sweaty and hatless, his hair looking as if it had never been combed. In other words, as gorgeous as ever. "I said I'd bring the mail home with me," Harper reminded him.

"I came to see you."

"Any reason?"

"To make sure you were behaving."

Relieved, Harper waved the postcard and headed into the lobby. "I'll put it on the bulletin board," she said, reading as she tacked it up.

Dear Everybody,

Thanks for the letters. We sure do miss you, but things here are fine. The baby's not due for another month, but we can't wait. Charlie and I are decorating the nursery together, mostly just to keep busy! All this time, we didn't know it, but the higher-ups at Mountaineer Equipment couldn't believe old Charlie would ever get married, much less be a doting daddy. Since they've been looking for a responsible family man, he got a promotion to Vice President of Service and Parts! Can you believe it? I also found a dude ranch near Pine Hills, so I hope Charlie, me and the baby can take our first vacation there.

We hope to see you again someday.

Love, Carrie Dawn

Gazing at the bulletin board, Harper smiled, feeling Macon's arms come around her. As she turned in his embrace, Mirabella made herself scarce. "So many babies," Harper murmured, "all coming at once."

Macon's eyes, full of emotion, settled on her full belly. "This time, I mean to be there for ours."

That was all it took. At the words, Harper's throat closed, feeling raw, and tears sprang to her eyes.

"Harper?"

"It's hormones." She defended herself.

"No, it's not." Tightening his arms around her so their hips locked, Macon filled her with the heat that they never failed to generate and that would never fail to thrill her. "Talk to me."

"I'm so sorry for what I did," she told him. "Nothing I do now can ever bring back the time you missed with Cordy."

"He had Bruce," said Macon gently. "Besides, we live together now." Macon chuckled. "He might be my son, but if he asks me one more time for a newer car, I may disown him."

She tried to smile at Macon's efforts to make her feel better, but she knew how he felt. "I'm sorry," she whispered again.

Macon's lips were hovering over hers, his breath so close it fluttered against her cheeks. Right before he lowered his mouth for a warm, sweet kiss, he whispered, "It's over now, Harper. What's past is past. All I care about is our future. I promise, I'll never bring up the past again."

And true to his word, Macon McCann never did.

Fantasies Inc.

An exclusive agency that caters to
intimate whims, provocative requests
and decadent desires...

Four lush island resorts waiting to
transport guests into a private world of
sensual adventures, erotic pleasures
and seductive passions...

A miniseries that will leave readers
breathless and yearning for more...

Don't miss:
#832 *SEDUCTIVE FANTASY* by Janelle Denison
Available May 2001

#836 *SECRET FANTASY* by Carly Phillips
Available June 2001

#840 *INTIMATE FANTASY* by Julie Kenner
Available July 2001

#844 *WILD FANTASY* by Janelle Denison
Available August 2001

Do you have a secret fantasy?

HARLEQUIN® *Temptation.*

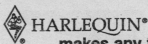

*Three sizzling love stories
by today's hottest writers
can be found in...*

Midnight Fantasies....

Feel the heat!

Available June 2001

MYSTERY LOVER—*Vicki Lewis Thompson*

When an unexpected storm hits, rancher Jonas Garfield
takes cover in a nearby cave...and finds himself seduced
senseless by an enigmatic temptress who refuses to tell him
her name. All he knows is that this sexy woman wants him.
And for Jonas, that's enough—for now....

AFTER HOURS—*Stephanie Bond*

Michael Pierce has always considered costume shop
owner Rebecca Valentine no more than an associate—
until he drops by her shop one night and witnesses the
mousy wallflower's transformation into a seductive siren.
Suddenly he's desperate to know her much better.
But which woman is the real Rebecca?

SHOW AND TELL—*Kimberly Raye*

A naughty lingerie party. A forbidden fantasy. When Texas
bad boy Dallas Jericho finds a slip of paper left over from
the party, he is surprised—and aroused—to discover that he
is good girl Laney Merriweather's wildest fantasy. So what
can he do but show the lady what she's been missing....

INDULGE IN A QUIET MOMENT
WITH HARLEQUIN

Get a FREE
Quiet Moments Bath Spa

with just two proofs of purchase from
any of our four special collector's editions in May.

Harlequin® is sure to make your time special this Mother's Day
with four special collector's editions featuring a short story
PLUS a complete novel packaged together in one volume!

Collection #1 Intrigue abounds in a collection featuring *New York Times*
bestselling author Barbara Delinsky and Kelsey Roberts.

Collection #2 Relationships? Weddings? Children? = *New York Times*
bestselling author Debbie Macomber and Tara Taylor Quinn
at their best!

Collection #3 Escape to the past with *New York Times* bestselling author
Heather Graham and Gayle Wilson.

Collection #4 Go West! With *New York Times* bestselling author
Joan Johnston and Vicki Lewis Thompson!

Plus Special Consumer Campaign!
Each of these four collector's editions will feature a
"FREE QUIET MOMENTS BATH SPA" offer.
See inside book in May for details.

Only from

HARLEQUIN®
Makes any time special ®

Don't miss out! Look for this exciting promotion on sale in May 2001,
at your favorite retail outlet.

Visit us at www.eHarlequin.com   PHNCP01